*Some Chains Are Invisible. Some Never Break.*

**Rowan Ashcliffe**

Copyright © 2025 by Rowan Ashcliffe

All rights reserved. No part of this book may be used or reproduced in any form whatsoever without written permission except in the case of brief quotations in critical articles or reviews.

First Edition: February 2025

# Table of Contents

Chapter 1 Blood and Binding ................................................... 1

Chapter 2 Shadows of the Past .................................................. 14

Chapter 3 The Council's Chains ................................................ 26

Chapter 4 Echoes of Old Magic ................................................ 37

Chapter 5 Tethered Fates ........................................................ 48

Chapter 6 The Black Library .................................................... 59

Chapter 7 Fractured Truths ...................................................... 71

Chapter 8 The Tether's Price ................................................... 81

Chapter 9 Chains and Choices .................................................. 93

Chapter 10 War Beneath the Veil ............................................. 103

Chapter 11 Crossing the Veil .................................................. 115

Chapter 12 The Heart of the Veil ............................................. 126

Chapter 13 A Bargain Written in Blood ..................................... 138

Chapter 14 The Breaking Point ................................................ 149

Chapter 15 Echoes After the Fall................................................ 161

Epilogue  The Shadow That Remains ........................................ 171

# Chapter 1
# Blood and Binding

Detective Selene Ward stepped through the door of apartment 47B, her boots striking the warped floorboards with a hollow thud. The scent hit her first—sharp and metallic, undercut by something sweeter, like rotting flowers left too long in stagnant water. The overhead bulb flickered with an unsteady pulse, casting jagged shadows across the peeling wallpaper. The air was thick, suffocating, as if the walls themselves were holding their breath.

Selene paused just inside the threshold, letting the weight of the scene settle over her like a second skin. Crime scenes always spoke if you listened closely enough. They whispered in the scuff marks on the floor, the disturbed dust on windowsills, the faintest drag of something heavy moved from one place to another. But this one didn't whisper. It screamed.

Her eyes moved with practiced precision, cataloging every detail without lingering too long. A shattered glass lay beneath an overturned coffee table, crimson droplets spider-webbing out from where the shards had bit into the hardwood. A discarded marriage contract lay crumpled near the base of a torn armchair, its parchment stained dark along the edges. But it was the bodies that drew her attention—a grotesque tableau on the faded floral couch.

The newlyweds were locked together, their limbs twisted in impossible angles, as if their joints had been wrenched apart and put back wrong. The bride's head lolled unnaturally, chin resting against her collarbone, her mouth frozen mid-scream. The groom's eyes stared straight ahead, glassy and wide, his hand still clutching her wrist with a grip that spoke of desperation, not affection.

Selene swallowed against the rising bile at the back of her throat. She'd seen plenty of bodies in her career, but this felt different. Wrong on a level that went beyond the physical.

She crouched beside them, her fingers hovering just above the brittle parchment on the floor. The marriage contract should have been pristine, its edges smooth, its sigils clear—a binding document both legal and magical. Instead, it was charred along one side, the intricate glyph that confirmed the union's permanence smeared into near nonexistence. Not faded. **Missing.** As if it had been ripped from reality itself.

Selene's gloved fingertips brushed the scorched edge. Cold—not the brittle stiffness of dried ink or burned paper, but something colder, like ice left too long in the dark. Her heart quickened.

"Another one," she murmured under her breath, the words tasting bitter on her tongue.

A floorboard creaked behind her, sharp in the oppressive silence. Selene's hand moved instinctively to the grip of her sidearm, fingers curling around the cool metal as she rose in one fluid motion. Her gaze snapped toward the source—a shadow flickering just beyond the doorway leading to the narrow hall. But when she moved closer, gun raised, the space was empty. Just the faint sway of a cracked mirror hanging crookedly on the wall.

Her reflection met her stare, distorted by the fissure running through the glass. For a heartbeat—just one—she thought she saw it move, not with her, but **independently**, like it blinked before she did.

Her breath hitched.

A voice cut through the tension.

"Detective?"

Selene didn't flinch. She lowered her weapon slightly, glancing over her shoulder to find Officer Mendez standing in the doorway, his expression tight, eyes darting nervously between her and the bodies.

"Forensics is on their way," Mendez said, shifting his weight from one foot to the other. His usual cocky demeanor was absent, replaced by something taut and uncertain. "What do you think?"

Selene straightened, sliding her weapon back into its holster with a soft click. She looked back at the couple, at the grotesque arch of the bride's spine, the tension still locked in her fingers.

"I think they didn't die peacefully," she said, her voice low, measured.

Mendez rubbed the back of his neck, his gaze skittering away from the corpses. "No forced entry. No signs of a struggle. It's like they just…" He hesitated, searching for the right words. "Did this to themselves."

Selene didn't respond. The idea hung in the air, absurd and fragile.

Her eyes drifted back to the contract. There was something else—a faint mark along the bottom corner, almost invisible beneath the charred edge. She crouched again, carefully prying the paper loose from where it had fused slightly to the floor. Beneath it, tucked under the bride's stiff fingers, was a small scrap of parchment, its edges burned, the ink smudged but still legible.

**Adrian Blackthorn.**

Selene's pulse surged.

Her hand clenched around the scrap instinctively, crumpling it before Mendez could catch a glimpse. She shoved it deep into the pocket of her coat, forcing her face into the mask of professionalism she wore like armor.

"Get the bodies to the morgue," she said, rising swiftly. "Full workup on toxicology. I want every detail—no matter how small."

Mendez nodded quickly, relief flickering across his face at the clear direction. He retreated, leaving Selene alone once more with the silence and the ghosts that lingered in the corners of the room.

She let out a slow breath, her fingers brushing the hidden scrap of parchment in her pocket. The name burned there, heavier than it should have been.

**Adrian.**

It had been months since she'd last seen him—longer since they'd spoken without words sharpened by anger. Their history was a fragile thing, stitched together with mistakes and regrets, buried beneath years of avoidance. But now, his name was here, tangled in a crime scene that didn't make sense, stitched into a narrative she didn't want to be part of.

Selene forced herself to move, stepping toward the cracked mirror one last time. She stared into it, studying the fractured reflection, waiting for it to betray her. For a moment, everything was still. Her face, her eyes, the faint flicker of the overhead bulb behind her.

But then—just as she turned to leave—**her reflection blinked.**

And she hadn't.

She didn't look back.

--------

Selene's boots echoed sharply against the tiled floor of the precinct, a rhythmic staccato that mirrored the pulse pounding in her ears. The florescent lights overhead flickered with an anemic buzz, casting sterile shadows across the rows of desks cluttered with case files, coffee cups, and the lingering scent of overworked ambition. She moved through the bullpen without acknowledging the curious glances that followed her. **They always looked at her like that**—with a mix of wariness and fascination, as if she carried her own storm cloud wherever she went. Maybe she did.

She didn't stop until she reached Captain Holt's office, his nameplate slightly askew, much like the man himself. Without knocking, she pushed the door open.

Holt glanced up from the paperwork littering his desk, his rugged face marked with lines carved by too many years of bad coffee and worse decisions. His piercing gaze met hers, and for a beat, he didn't say anything.

"You look like hell," he muttered finally, leaning back in his chair and crossing his arms over his chest.

"Feeling's mutual," Selene shot back, slamming the door shut behind her.

She tossed a thin folder onto his desk, the crime scene photos spilling out—bodies twisted in grotesque postures, blood staining the cheap upholstery like dark flowers blooming across fabric. Holt didn't flinch. He'd seen worse—or at least pretended he had.

"Another one," Selene said flatly.

Holt's brow furrowed as he picked up one of the photos. "Same MO?"

"Exactly the same," she replied, pacing the small office like a caged animal. "No forced entry. No struggle. Contracts compromised."

Holt grunted. "Impossible."

Selene stopped, her jaw tightening. "Apparently not."

She reached into her coat pocket and pulled out the scorched scrap of parchment, the name **Adrian Blackthorn** faint but unmistakable against the burnt edges. She slapped it onto his desk, watching his face carefully.

Holt's reaction was subtle—a slight narrowing of his eyes, a twitch in his jaw—but she didn't miss it.

"Well, that's a hell of a coincidence," he said after a beat, his voice too casual.

"I don't believe in coincidences," Selene replied, her tone sharp enough to cut glass.

Holt set the photo down and leaned forward, his elbows resting on the battered wood of his desk. "You think he's involved?"

"I don't know," Selene admitted, which felt like a failure in itself. She hated not knowing. "But his name was at the scene. That's not nothing."

Holt rubbed a hand over his face, sighing heavily. "You spoken to him yet?"

"Not yet."

"Then don't."

Selene blinked. "What?"

Holt's gaze hardened. "You heard me. Leave it alone, Ward."

Selene's laugh was short and humorless. "Since when do I leave things alone?"

Holt slammed his hand down on the desk, making the coffee cup near the edge jump. "This isn't about your damn pride, Selene. Blackthorn's got ties to the Veil Council. Deep ones. You start poking around, and they'll poke back harder."

"I can handle it."

"You think you can," Holt shot back, standing now, his voice low and rough like gravel. "But the Council doesn't play by the rules. Hell, they write the rules. You go after Blackthorn, and you won't just be risking your badge."

Selene stepped closer, her face inches from his. "Maybe I'm not worried about the badge."

Holt stared at her, his jaw clenched so tightly she could see the muscle twitching. Then he exhaled sharply, stepping back and raking a hand through his graying hair.

"Damn it, Selene. This isn't just another case."

"No," she agreed softly, her fingers brushing the parchment still on the desk. "It's not."

Silence stretched between them, thick with everything they weren't saying. Finally, Holt shook his head, his shoulders sagging with defeat.

"You're gonna do what you're gonna do," he muttered, sinking back into his chair. "Just… be careful."

Selene didn't reply. She turned and left the office, her heart pounding in time with her footsteps as she made her way down the hall. But the echoes of Holt's warning followed her, threading through the noise like a whisper she couldn't shake.

She paused by the cracked mirror hanging near the stairwell, its surface clouded with age and neglect. She stared at her reflection, the harsh fluorescent lights casting shadows under her eyes, making her look older, harder.

For a moment—just a breath—she thought she saw it blink.

And she hadn't.

Selene turned away before her reflection could do anything else.

Selene's apartment greeted her with the same cold detachment it always did—bare walls, minimal furniture, and a single flickering bulb dangling from the ceiling like a tired sentinel. The faint hum of the city beyond her windows seeped through the thin glass, muffled and distant, a heartbeat that didn't quite sync with her own. She locked the door behind her with an unnecessary amount of force, the deadbolt sliding into place with a satisfying *click*.

She tossed her coat over the back of the worn-out chair and pulled the scorched scrap of parchment from her pocket. The name stared back at her like it had been etched into her memory long before it ever touched ink—**Adrian Blackthorn.** The letters were uneven, the edges of the parchment singed, as if it had barely survived whatever force had claimed the lives of the couple on that crimson-streaked couch.

Selene sank into the chair, her elbows resting on her knees, the parchment dangling from her fingertips. She should've thrown it away. Hell, she should've logged it into evidence like any good detective would. But that name… it was more than evidence. It was a fracture line running through the brittle shell of her carefully constructed life.

She traced the edge of the parchment with her thumb, feeling the faint ridges where the paper had burned. Scorch marks. Not from fire—not the kind she recognized. The pattern was too deliberate, like veins spreading out from a single, precise point.

A sigil once burned here? Maybe. But if so, it was long gone, devoured by whatever darkness had left its mark.

Her mind drifted to Adrian—his sharp smile, the way he used to call her name like it was a secret, and the cold emptiness he left behind when he disappeared into the web of the Veil Council. She had buried those memories deep, under layers of resentment and indifference. Or so she thought.

Her phone vibrated on the table, jolting her from the spiral. She grabbed it, expecting maybe Mendez or even Holt with an update. But the screen was blank—no calls, no messages. Just her own reflection staring back at her in the dark glass.

She frowned, setting the phone down slowly. The room felt heavier somehow, like the shadows had thickened while she wasn't looking. She rubbed her eyes, exhaustion gnawing at the edges of her thoughts.

Then she heard it.

A whisper. Soft. Just her name.

"Selene…"

She froze, her breath hitching. It wasn't loud. It wasn't even distinct. But it was there—just enough to send a shiver crawling down her spine.

She turned slowly, her eyes scanning the dim apartment. Nothing. Just the faint hum of the city outside and the soft creak of her own breath in the silence.

"Get it together," she muttered under her breath, pushing herself up from the chair.

But as she moved past the cracked mirror hanging in the narrow hallway, she saw it—*movement.*

She stopped. Her heart raced.

Her reflection stood still, but something behind it shifted—a shadow where there shouldn't be one, flickering like a flame caught in a draft. She spun around, fists clenched, but the hallway was empty. Just walls and shadows. Nothing more.

She stared at the space for a long moment, her pulse slowly returning to something resembling normal. Then she turned back to the mirror, stepping closer.

Her reflection met her gaze with dark, tired eyes. But it wasn't right. Not exactly.

She raised her hand.

The reflection followed.

She tilted her head.

The reflection did the same.

But then it blinked—*before she did.*

Selene stumbled back, her breath sharp in her chest. She looked around again, half-expecting something to be there this time. But the apartment remained as empty and hollow as it always had been.

She didn't sleep that night.

Instead, she sat at her small kitchen table, the parchment laid out in front of her, the faint scorch marks like veins connecting dots she couldn't see yet. She traced them with her fingertip, her mind racing with possibilities she didn't want to entertain.

This wasn't just a killing. It wasn't random.

It was a message.

And it was meant for her.

# Chapter 2
# Shadows of the Past

The rain had started sometime after midnight, leaving the city streets slick and shimmering under the weak glow of streetlights. Selene stood across from the modest building that Adrian Blackthorn called home—a decaying relic tucked between newer, shinier structures, like it had been forgotten by time itself. The windows were dark except for a faint sliver of light spilling from the narrow gap beneath the door on the third floor. He was home. She'd known he would be. People like Adrian never strayed far from their shadows.

She crossed the street with purpose, her footsteps muffled by the wet pavement. The building's door groaned in protest as she pushed it open, the narrow staircase inside bathed in stale air and the faint scent of old cigarette smoke embedded in the walls. She didn't bother with subtlety. If he didn't know she was coming, he wasn't the man she remembered.

Selene's knuckles rapped against his door twice—sharp, decisive. No answer.

She waited three seconds before her patience frayed. Reaching down, she tested the handle. Locked, of course. But locks were just suggestions in the world they lived in. A swift twist of her wrist, a little pressure with a thin blade she kept tucked in her boot, and the door clicked open.

Adrian was exactly where she expected—leaning casually against the edge of his desk, a glass of something amber in his hand, as if he'd been expecting her all along.

"Well," he drawled, lifting the glass slightly in greeting. "If it isn't Detective Selene Ward. Breaking and entering now? Must be a slow night."

Selene stepped inside, shutting the door with her foot. The apartment was as sparse as she remembered—bookshelves cluttered with old tomes, maps pinned to the walls, and a faint trace of incense lingering in the air, unable to mask the underlying scent of something older. Something like burnt parchment.

"Your name was at a crime scene," Selene said without preamble, pulling the scorched scrap from her pocket and tossing it onto the table between them.

Adrian didn't flinch. He set his glass down gently, his fingers brushing against the parchment with a fleeting touch, as if it might bite.

"I see you've been busy," he murmured, his tone light but his eyes sharp.

"Don't play games, Adrian. The victims were found twisted like broken dolls, their marriage contract burnt—missing its sigil. And this—" she jabbed a finger at the scrap—"was tucked under the bride's hand. Explain."

He exhaled through his nose, not quite a sigh, more an acknowledgment of inevitability. "It's not as simple as you think."

"Try me."

He pushed off the desk, stepping closer, his movements smooth, deliberate. "You think I had something to do with it?"

"I think your name doesn't end up at crime scenes by accident."

Adrian's jaw tensed, the easy charm slipping just enough to reveal the tension underneath. "I didn't kill them, Selene."

"Then what do you know?"

He glanced at the parchment again, then away, as if looking at it too long might unravel something inside him. "It's not about them. It's about what they were part of."

Selene folded her arms across her chest, her heart thudding against the cage of her ribs. "The Veil Council?"

Adrian gave a dry, humorless laugh. "Always so quick. Yes. The Council."

She stepped forward, closing the distance between them. "Then start talking."

Adrian met her gaze, his expression shifting from casual to something colder, darker. "You're poking at things you don't understand, Selene. The Council doesn't care about justice or truth. They care about control. Contracts, sigils, laws—they're just tools. The real power lies beneath all that, in places you've never been. Places you don't want to go."

Selene's jaw tightened. "I've been to darker places than you think."

His eyes softened briefly, a flicker of something unspoken passing between them. Regret? Nostalgia? It didn't matter. She crushed it beneath her heel like the fragile thing it was.

"I need answers, not cryptic warnings," she snapped.

Adrian turned away, running a hand through his dark hair, his fingers lingering at the back of his neck as if trying to hold something in. "The victims," he said finally, his voice quieter now, almost reluctant. "They were part of something… experimental. The Council's been modifying the contracts—testing boundaries they shouldn't be testing. Removing sigils isn't supposed to be possible. Not without—" He stopped himself, shaking his head.

"Not without what?"

He looked at her then, really looked, and she felt the weight of it like a hand around her throat.

"Not without breaking the soul it's bound to."

Silence settled between them, thick and suffocating.

Selene swallowed hard, her mind racing. "So why your name? What does this have to do with you?"

Adrian smiled, but it didn't reach his eyes. "Everything, unfortunately."

She wanted to shake him, to force the truth out of him. But she knew Adrian. He'd only give what he wanted, when he wanted. Press too hard, and he'd shut down completely.

She stepped back, her pulse still racing. "If you're lying to me—"

"I'm not."

She studied him for another long moment, then turned toward the door.

"Selene," he called after her.

She paused, hand on the knob, not looking back.

"Be careful," he said softly. "The Council doesn't like loose ends."

She didn't respond. Just walked out, the door clicking shut behind her. But his words followed her down the hall, an echo she couldn't shake.

--------

The precinct was a labyrinth of buzzing fluorescent lights and voices layered over the hum of tired machines. Selene pushed through the front doors, the warmth of the place doing little to shake the cold that had settled under her skin after her encounter with Adrian. She moved through the corridors with mechanical precision, each step echoing faintly against the linoleum floors.

Her desk sat in the far corner, cluttered with case files, a half-empty cup of cold coffee, and a few scattered notes she hadn't bothered to organize. Mendez was already there, hunched over the forensic reports like they held the answers to the universe. His tie was loosened, his sleeves rolled up, and a grim expression carved into his usually easygoing face.

"You look like you've seen a ghost," Mendez muttered without looking up as Selene approached.

Selene ignored the comment, dropping into the chair opposite him. "What do we have?"

Mendez sighed, flipping a page. "Inconclusive. That's the official term. But I'd call it something else."

Selene arched a brow. "Like what?"

"Like bullshit," he said, tossing the report onto the desk with enough force to send a few papers sliding. "No fingerprints, no foreign DNA, nothing under the victims' nails. The bodies show signs of extreme stress—muscle tearing, ligature-like bruising—but no actual restraints. It's like… like they fought against something that wasn't there."

Selene leaned forward, her fingers drumming against the desk. "And the sigils?"

Mendez shook his head. "That's the weirdest part. They weren't tampered with. They're just… gone. Like they were never there in the first place."

Selene felt a chill that had nothing to do with the air conditioning. She pulled the burned scrap of parchment from her coat pocket, laying it on the desk beside the report.

Mendez squinted at it. "What's that?"

"Found it at the scene. Had a chat with someone whose name was on it."

Mendez glanced up, his expression sharp. "And?"

"And nothing. He's not talking."

Mendez frowned, picking up the parchment carefully, as if it might bite. "This feel off to you?"

Selene didn't answer. She didn't need to.

Mendez sighed again, leaning back in his chair. "You know, this isn't the first case like this."

Selene's gaze snapped to him. "What?"

"I've been digging," he said, rifling through a stack of files. He pulled one free and slid it across the desk to her. "Three months ago—same M.O. A couple found dead in their apartment. No signs of forced entry, no struggle. Contract missing its sigil."

Selene opened the file, her eyes scanning the photos. The scene was eerily similar—bodies twisted, faces frozen in silent agony. She flipped through the pages, her heart pounding harder with each one.

"There's more," Mendez continued, pulling out another file. "Six months before that. Different city, same story."

Selene felt the pieces clicking together, forming a pattern she didn't like.

"These aren't random," she whispered, more to herself than to Mendez.

"No," he agreed. "They're not."

Selene stared at the photos, her mind racing. The missing sigils, the lack of physical evidence, the connection to Adrian—all threads in a web she was only just beginning to see.

She stood abruptly, grabbing the files. "I need to see the captain."

Mendez watched her go, his face a mixture of concern and curiosity. "Be careful, Ward," he called after her. "This feels bigger than it looks."

Selene didn't respond. She didn't need to.

She already knew.

---

The night air was thick with mist, the city's glow bleeding into the fog like a bruise spreading under the skin. Selene found herself standing once again outside the door of apartment 47B, the faded number dangling loosely, casting a crooked shadow in the dim hallway light. She hadn't planned to come back—not officially, not even consciously—but something pulled her here, an itch beneath her skin that logic couldn't scratch.

The door creaked open easily under her hand, the lock already compromised from earlier. The apartment greeted her with the same oppressive silence, the stale scent of decay and burnt parchment lingering like a memory refusing to fade. She stepped inside, her footsteps softer this time, as if the walls themselves might be listening.

The living room remained untouched. The crimson stains had darkened, seeping into the wood, stubborn reminders of life violently unmade. The crime scene tape fluttered slightly in the draft from the cracked window, a pale echo of life in a room filled with echoes of death.

Selene's gaze drifted to the mirror.

It hung crookedly on the wall, fractured lines spider-webbing across its surface. In the dim light, the cracks seemed deeper, more pronounced, like veins pulsing beneath glass skin. She moved toward it slowly, her reflection warping with each step until it no longer felt like her own.

She stopped just a foot away, staring at the distorted image. Her face stared back—tired eyes, sharp cheekbones shadowed under the flickering bulb—but something was off. The reflection didn't match her movements perfectly. There was a delay, slight but undeniable. She tilted her head to the left; her reflection followed but with a heartbeat's hesitation.

A chill coiled around her spine.

"Selene…"

The whisper was soft, curling through the silence like smoke. It wasn't in the room. It was in the mirror.

Her heart thudded, heavy and out of rhythm. She reached out instinctively, her fingers hovering just above the cracked surface. The glass felt cold, even without contact, radiating a chill that seeped into her skin.

Then it moved.

Her reflection blinked—but she hadn't.

She stumbled back, her hand dropping to the grip of her sidearm. The room around her blurred, the shadows stretching, shifting unnaturally, bending toward her like fingers reaching through the dark.

The mirror darkened, her reflection fading until all that remained were her eyes—no, not hers. The shape was wrong. The color too dark, like ink bleeding into water. And then the whisper came again, louder this time.

"Selene… you can't outrun it."

She clenched her jaw, shaking her head. "Get a grip," she muttered, grounding herself in the familiar weight of her weapon, her badge, her breath. But the air felt heavier now, thick with something she couldn't name.

The mirror's surface rippled.

She squeezed her eyes shut, counting to three, grounding herself in reality—the scrape of her boots on the floor, the faint buzz of the flickering light, the steady rhythm of her heartbeat.

When she opened her eyes, the mirror was just glass again. Cracked, broken, but ordinary.

She exhaled shakily, sliding her weapon back into its holster. The urge to flee scratched at the edges of her mind, but she forced herself to stay, to think. Fear was a luxury she couldn't afford.

Her gaze drifted to the corner where the marriage contract had been found. She knelt, running her fingers over the floorboards, now cold beneath her touch. There were faint scorch marks here, barely visible, as if the fire had burned not on the surface but within it, seared into the very grain of the wood.

A message. Not just a crime scene—**a message meant for her.**

She didn't know how she knew that, but the certainty settled into her bones, undeniable.

As she stood to leave, her eyes flicked back to the mirror one last time.

Her reflection smiled.

But she wasn't.

# Chapter 3
# The Council's Chains

Selene didn't like being summoned, especially not by someone like **Eleanor Vale**. The woman had a reputation that preceded her—a sharp mind wrapped in silk, with eyes that could slice deeper than any blade. But here she was, standing in front of the glass doors of an upscale café tucked into the heart of Nightrift's financial district, feeling like she'd just stepped into enemy territory.

The café was all polished chrome and minimalist design, the type of place where people discussed mergers, not murders. Selene spotted Eleanor immediately, seated at a corner table, her posture immaculate, fingers wrapped delicately around a porcelain cup. She was dressed in dark, tailored attire that whispered authority without screaming it. Her platinum hair was pulled into a sleek knot, and her expression was unreadable, as if carved from marble.

Selene approached, dropping into the seat across from her without waiting for an invitation.

"Detective Ward," Eleanor greeted, her voice smooth as velvet with an undertone of steel. "Punctuality. I appreciate that."

"I wasn't exactly given a choice," Selene replied, leaning back, arms crossed. "You wanted to talk. So talk."

Eleanor smiled faintly, as if Selene's bluntness amused her. "Straight to the point. Refreshing. I understand you've been… involved in the Blackthorn investigation."

Selene's jaw tensed. "It's not an 'investigation' into him. His name showed up at a crime scene. That's not something I ignore."

Eleanor's fingers tapped lightly against her cup. "Adrian has a complicated history. His ties to the Veil Council run deep. You'd do well to tread carefully."

Selene leaned forward, her eyes narrowing. "Is that a threat?"

"Consider it friendly advice," Eleanor replied smoothly. "The Council prefers certain matters remain undisturbed."

Selene snorted. "I don't work for the Council."

"No," Eleanor agreed softly. "But you work around them. And that distinction can be dangerous."

Selene didn't flinch. "I'm not here for cryptic warnings. What do you know about the missing sigils?"

Eleanor's smile faded slightly, her gaze sharpening. "You think this is about the sigils?"

"I know it is," Selene shot back. "People are dead. Their marriage contracts were tampered with—ripped apart like paper. That's not just some bureaucratic glitch."

Eleanor was silent for a moment, studying Selene as if deciding how much truth she was willing to part with. Then she leaned in slightly, her voice dropping to a near whisper.

"The contracts aren't just legal documents," she said. "They're... bindings. Agreements that go beyond ink and parchment."

Selene frowned. "Bindings? You mean magical?"

Eleanor's lips twitched. "Magic is a simplistic term. Let's call it... a force. One that requires balance."

Selene's mind raced. "So, when a sigil disappears—"

"It's not just paperwork being erased," Eleanor finished. "It's a rupture. A tear in something far older and more fragile than any contract."

Selene's pulse quickened. "Why would someone do that?"

"Power," Eleanor said simply. "Control."

Selene leaned back, her heart pounding. "And Adrian's involved?"

Eleanor hesitated, then gave a small nod. "In ways even he doesn't fully understand."

Selene absorbed that, her mind piecing together fragments of evidence, memories, and warnings.

"If you're so concerned," Selene said after a beat, "why tell me?"

Eleanor's smile returned, thin and sharp. "Because sometimes the only way to protect something is to make sure the right person is looking at it."

"And you think that's me?"

Eleanor's gaze didn't waver. "I know it is."

Selene stood, her chair scraping against the polished floor. "I don't play games, Vale."

Eleanor's smile lingered. "Everyone plays the game, Detective. Some just don't realize it."

Selene left without another word, but Eleanor's voice echoed in her mind long after she was gone.

--------

Selene's apartment was dark when she returned, but she didn't bother with the lights. The dim glow from the streetlights outside was enough as she dropped her keys on the counter and headed straight for the stack of case files spread across her coffee table. They looked like any other homicide reports—routine, sterile, clinical. But she knew better now.

She'd spent hours combing through archived records at the precinct, pulling strings, calling in favors, digging into cases that had been conveniently buried under layers of bureaucratic red tape. The connections were subtle, but they were there—families with ties to the **Veil Council**, victims whose deaths were marked by the same eerie absence of sigils, their contracts eerily scrubbed clean.

Selene flipped through the files, her fingers tracing over names and dates. Each one whispered the same truth: **this wasn't an isolated case.** It was a pattern.

Her phone buzzed, vibrating against the table's surface like an insect trapped under glass. She glanced at the screen—**Captain Holt.**

She answered without thinking, her voice rough from hours of silence. "Ward."

"Where the hell are you?" Holt's voice was sharp, edged with frustration. "You didn't check in after your meeting with Vale."

Selene rubbed the back of her neck, her muscles tense. "I've been working."

"Working on what? Ignoring direct orders?"

Selene's jaw tightened. "Since when do we ignore evidence?"

There was a pause on the other end, filled with the static hum of the city's background noise bleeding through Holt's end of the line.

"Where are you?" he asked again, quieter this time.

Selene didn't answer. Instead, she flipped to the next file, her eyes narrowing at the name highlighted in red—**Mara Ellison.** Another victim. Another missing sigil. But this file was different. The official cause of death was listed as **"cardiac arrest,"** yet the crime scene photos told a different story—her body twisted unnaturally, eyes wide with terror.

"Holt," Selene said, her voice low. "How many cases like this have been buried?"

"Selene—"

"How many?" she snapped, slamming the file shut.

Holt exhaled sharply. "It's not that simple."

"It's exactly that simple," she shot back. "These people didn't just drop dead. Their contracts were wiped clean, their lives erased like they never mattered. And every one of them had ties to the Council."

"That's not your jurisdiction," Holt growled. "You're not a damn conspiracy theorist. You're a detective. Follow the evidence, not your gut."

"I am following the evidence," she hissed. "It's just leading somewhere you don't want to see."

Silence again. Then Holt's voice dropped to a near whisper, rough and tired. "You're poking a hornet's nest, Ward."

"Good," she snapped. "Maybe it's time someone got stung."

She hung up before he could respond, her heart racing. The anger felt good. It was better than fear.

She grabbed the files and spread them out across the floor, connecting names, dates, and locations. Red strings of scribbled notes crisscrossed between the papers, tracing the invisible threads that tied everything together.

**The Council. The contracts. The missing sigils.**

And in the center of it all, like a black hole pulling everything inward—**Adrian Blackthorn.**

Selene stared at the web of connections, her mind buzzing with questions she wasn't sure she wanted answers to. But she couldn't stop now. She was in too deep. And maybe that's exactly where she needed to be.

--------

The night had swallowed the city whole, casting Nightrift in shades of gray and black, where even the streetlights seemed hesitant to pierce the fog curling through narrow alleys and empty streets. Selene's footsteps echoed against damp pavement, steady and deliberate, the rhythmic sound the only heartbeat in the suffocating silence around her. The air was thick, clinging to her skin like damp velvet, blurring edges, smudging shapes—perfect cover for someone who didn't want to be seen.

But Selene had felt the presence long before she'd heard it. A prickle at the back of her neck, the faintest whisper of footsteps a breath out of sync with her own. Someone was following her.

She didn't look back.

Instead, she let her pace slow slightly, her body loose, casual—a predator pretending to be prey. She turned down an alley, the walls closing in on either side, graffiti-streaked bricks slick with condensation. Her reflection winked back at her from puddles scattered like dark mirrors, distorted, fragmented.

Halfway down the alley, she stopped.

The footsteps behind her stopped too.

Selene smiled without humor, her hand drifting to the grip of her sidearm, the motion smooth, instinctual. She didn't draw—not yet. She wanted to see who had the nerve to follow her in the open like this.

Without turning around, she spoke, her voice low but cutting through the fog like a blade.

"You're not very good at this."

Silence.

Then, a soft shuffle. Deliberate footsteps now, approaching slowly. No attempt to hide. Whoever it was wanted her to know they were there.

Selene pivoted smoothly, her weapon drawn and steady before the figure could take another step.

The person who emerged from the shadows was wrapped in a long, dark coat, the hood pulled low, obscuring most of their face. But there was no mistaking the way they moved—confident, controlled, like someone who'd spent years mastering the art of being dangerous without having to prove it.

Selene's finger hovered near the trigger. "This is the part where you explain why you're following me."

The figure stopped a few paces away, raising their hands slightly, palms empty, fingers slender and gloved.

"No need for that," the figure said, the voice smooth, androgynous, carrying an accent that hinted at places Selene had never been. "If I wanted to hurt you, you wouldn't have heard me."

Selene didn't lower her weapon. "Try me."

A soft chuckle, then the figure pulled back the hood, revealing sharp features framed by dark hair tied neatly at the nape of their neck. Their eyes were the unsettling part—pale gray, almost colorless, and too still, like storm clouds that had forgotten how to move.

"Name's irrelevant," they said, tilting their head slightly. "But the message is important."

Selene's grip didn't waver. "Then you'd better talk fast."

The figure's smile was thin, humorless. "You're poking where you shouldn't, Detective Ward. The Council doesn't appreciate curious minds."

Selene's lips curled into something resembling a smirk. "Good. I don't appreciate veiled threats."

"No veil here," they replied smoothly. "Consider this direct. Walk away from the Blackthorn case. Forget the missing sigils. Leave the past buried."

Selene's jaw tightened. "Or what?"

The enforcer stepped closer, ignoring the gun still aimed at their chest. Their voice dropped to a whisper, sharp and cold.

"Or you'll find out how thin the line is between investigator and corpse."

Selene's finger twitched, but she didn't shoot. Not yet.

Instead, she lowered the gun slightly, just enough to signal she wasn't scared—but not enough to pretend she wasn't ready.

"You tell the Council this," she said, her voice steady as stone. "I don't bury the truth. I dig it up. And I'm just getting started."

The enforcer's smile faded completely, leaving behind only that eerie stillness in their eyes.

"A shame," they murmured before turning, disappearing into the fog as silently as they'd come.

Selene stood there for a long moment after they were gone, her heart pounding, adrenaline sharp in her veins.

But beneath it, something colder had settled.

Not fear.

Resolve.

# Chapter 4
# Echoes of Old Magic

Selene's apartment was suffocatingly silent when she returned, the dim city lights filtering through half-closed blinds, casting thin slashes of gold across the dusty floorboards. She dropped her coat onto the chair by the door, her body moving out of habit while her mind churned, a storm brewing behind her tired eyes. The confrontation with the Council's enforcer echoed in her head, not as a threat, but as an affirmation—**she was getting too close.**

She made her way to the small, battered desk shoved into the corner of the room. Its drawers were filled with old case files, scattered notes, and memories she had long since tried to forget. But it was the hidden compartment beneath the bottom drawer that she reached for now, fingers deftly sliding against the false panel until it popped free with a soft *click*.

Inside, wrapped in aged parchment and tied with a thin black ribbon, was her own secret—the one she'd buried under layers of denial and stubbornness.

A **contract.**

Her name etched in precise, almost delicate script at the top: **Selene Ward.**

She unwrapped it carefully, her breath shallow. The paper felt brittle under her touch, the once-vibrant sigil in the corner now faded, its intricate lines barely visible. It had been flawless once, binding, permanent—or so she thought.

Now, it was decaying.

Her fingers trembled slightly as she traced the faint outlines of the sigil, a cold dread blooming in her chest. It matched the missing marks from the crime scenes, the same strange fading that shouldn't be possible.

Not without something… breaking.

A sharp knock at the door pulled her from the spiral. She shoved the contract back into the compartment, covering it hastily before standing. Her heart was still racing as she opened the door to find **Mendez** standing there, holding a file in one hand and a six-pack in the other.

"I brought bribes," he said, holding up the beer with a crooked smile. But his eyes were sharp, reading her tension like an open book.

Selene stepped aside, letting him in without a word. Mendez made himself at home, dropping the file on the coffee table and cracking open a beer.

"You look like you've seen a ghost," he said, taking a sip before settling into the worn armchair.

Selene didn't respond. Instead, she poured herself a glass of water, her fingers still shaking slightly. Mendez watched her over the rim of his bottle, his smile fading.

"What's going on, Ward?"

She considered lying, brushing it off with some sarcastic remark. But the weight of the contract hidden just a few feet away felt heavier than usual.

"I found something," she said finally, her voice quieter than she intended. "Something I didn't expect."

Mendez raised an eyebrow. "You? Not expecting something? That's a first."

She shot him a look, but there was no real heat behind it.

"Seriously," he said, leaning forward. "Talk to me."

Selene hesitated, then nodded slightly, deciding how much she could say without unraveling completely.

"Those contracts," she began, her gaze fixed on the condensation dripping down the side of her glass. "They're not just legal documents. They're… more."

Mendez frowned. "Like what? Some kind of magical bullshit?"

"Something like that."

He stared at her for a long moment, then sighed. "You're serious."

Selene nodded, her throat tight.

"And Adrian?" Mendez asked, his voice softer now. "Where does he fit into this?"

Selene's chest ached at the sound of his name, a thousand memories flooding her mind—arguments in dimly lit apartments, whispered promises in the dark, the look in his eyes the day he walked away.

"He's connected," she said quietly. "More than I want to admit."

Mendez didn't push, just nodded, accepting her words without the need for more.

After a long silence, he stood, grabbing his file. "I pulled some reports. Found another case—same M.O., same missing sigil. Thought you'd want to see it."

He handed her the file, and she took it with a small nod of thanks.

As he left, the apartment felt even emptier than before.

Selene sat back down, her fingers brushing against the hidden compartment once more, the faded sigil a ghost beneath her skin.

--------

The narrow alley where **Elias Gray** operated wasn't listed on any city map. It was tucked between crumbling buildings like a scar the city had tried to forget. Selene's boots echoed softly against the cracked pavement, the faint scent of rust and burnt sage lingering in the cool evening air. A crooked sign swung above a battered door—**"GRAY'S CURIOSITIES"** etched faintly, almost as if the name itself didn't want to be remembered.

Selene knocked twice, the wood splintering slightly under her knuckles. No answer.

She tried again, her patience already thin.

Finally, the door creaked open a sliver, revealing a single sharp gray eye peering through the gap.

"Detective Ward," Elias's voice was a raspy drawl, threaded with annoyance and curiosity. "To what do I owe the pleasure of this completely unannounced visit?"

Selene didn't wait for an invitation. She shoved the door open and stepped inside, her gaze sweeping over the cluttered space. Books piled like precarious towers, strange artifacts littered every surface—bones, rusted keys, glass jars filled with things better left unidentified.

"I need answers," she said simply, letting the door creak shut behind her.

Elias sighed dramatically, stepping into the dim light. He was tall, angular, with silver-streaked hair tied at the nape of his neck and a perpetual look of having seen too much. His coat was threadbare, sleeves rolled up to reveal inked symbols running along his forearms like living veins.

"Answers come with a price," Elias murmured, brushing dust off an ancient-looking book. "And you're not exactly my favorite client."

Selene pulled the folded parchment from her coat pocket and tossed it onto the nearest table. "Name your price."

Elias's expression shifted the moment he saw the contract. His fingers hesitated before picking it up, as if touching it might leave a mark.

"Where did you get this?" he asked, voice lower now, the humor drained away.

"A crime scene," Selene replied. "Victims dead, bodies twisted. Their marriage contract missing its sigil. This one's mine."

Elias's eyes snapped up to hers. For the first time, genuine concern flickered across his face.

"You're playing with forces you don't understand."

Selene stepped closer, her jaw tight. "Then explain it to me."

Elias carefully unfolded the parchment, his fingers tracing the faded sigil, his brow furrowing deeper with each passing second.

"This isn't just a contract," he whispered. "It's a tether."

"To what?"

Elias glanced at her, his expression grim. "To something ancient. Older than the Council, older than the systems built around it. These contracts were never meant to be legal documents—they're **anchors**."

"Anchors to what?"

Elias hesitated, then finally said, "To things that feed on connection. Emotion. Bonds between people. The Council didn't create this system—they just learned how to control it."

Selene's pulse quickened. "And the fading sigils?"

Elias set the parchment down gently, as if afraid it might shatter. "When a sigil fades, it means the tether is breaking. But it doesn't just affect the contract—it affects the soul it's bound to. The victims… they weren't just killed. They were **unraveled**."

Selene swallowed hard, her mind racing. "Can it be stopped?"

Elias met her gaze, his eyes dark. "Maybe. But the cost—" he paused, shaking his head. "The cost is never what you expect."

Selene didn't flinch. She'd paid plenty already.

She picked up the parchment, folding it carefully before slipping it back into her coat.

"Thanks for the warning," she said, turning toward the door.

Elias's voice followed her as she left. "Be careful, Detective. The deeper you dig, the closer you get to something that's been buried for a reason."

Selene didn't respond.

Some things needed to be unearthed.

--------

The door to **Elias Gray's** shop creaked shut behind Selene, cutting off the stale, dusty warmth of the cluttered interior and replacing it with the cold bite of Nightrift's night air. The streets were quieter than usual, muffled under a heavy fog that crept in from the harbor, thick and slow like fingers spreading across the city. She pulled her coat tighter around herself, but the chill she felt wasn't from the weather.

Elias's words echoed in her mind, each syllable sinking deeper than she wanted to admit. **"A tether… something ancient… the cost is never what you expect."** She didn't need riddles. She needed facts. Answers. But answers always had a price, and Selene was beginning to feel the debt piling up.

She moved quickly, her footsteps tapping out a steady rhythm against cracked pavement. The city felt hollow tonight—buildings like empty husks, shadows stretching too long, too dark. She told herself it was just the fog, the exhaustion, the weight of everything pressing down at once.

But then she heard it.

A faint whisper.

At first, she thought it was just the wind snaking through the narrow alleys. But no—it was sharper than that. *Closer.*

"Selene…"

She froze mid-step. The voice was familiar, though she couldn't place it. Her hand instinctively moved to the inside of her coat, fingers brushing against the folded parchment Elias had studied with such grim reverence. Its presence was a pulse against her skin, faint but insistent, like a second heartbeat.

She turned slowly, scanning the fog-drenched street. Empty. No footsteps but her own. No movement except the sluggish drift of mist curling around lampposts.

Then she saw them.

Figures, emerging from the fog—**shadows wearing faces she recognized.**

Mendez's eyes—wide, lifeless.

Captain Holt's voice, echoing from nowhere and everywhere. *"You should've walked away, Selene."*

And worse—faces from cases long closed. Victims she couldn't save. Their mouths twisted in silent screams, their hands reaching for her, fingers outstretched like brittle claws.

Selene stumbled back, her breath coming in ragged gasps. She blinked hard, trying to ground herself, to remind herself this wasn't real.

But it *felt* real.

The pavement beneath her feet cracked, spiderweb fissures racing out like fractures in glass. The world tilted, shadows bleeding into light, distorting the street into something warped and wrong. She reached for the wall beside her to steady herself, but her hand passed through it, meeting only cold, empty air.

The voices grew louder, overlapping—a cacophony of accusations.

*"You failed us."*
*"You're the reason we're gone."*
*"You can't outrun it."*

Selene squeezed her eyes shut, her nails digging into her palms. *This isn't real. It isn't real.*

But the weight of it crushed down on her like it was.

Her knees buckled. She hit the ground hard, her palms scraping against rough concrete, but she barely felt the sting. Her trembling fingers clutched the parchment inside her coat, pulling it out like it was a lifeline. The brittle edges crumpled under her grip, the faded sigil pulsing faintly, like it was alive.

And that's when she realized—**it wasn't just following her.**

It was *inside* her.

The darkness wasn't something she could fight with bullets or logic. It had threaded itself through her, tangled in her memories, her regrets, her very soul. She was the tether Elias had warned about.

As the visions swirled around her, Selene pressed the parchment against her chest, her heartbeat frantic beneath it. She whispered to herself, the words ragged and broken.

*"This isn't real. This isn't real…"*

But even as she said it, part of her knew—

**It was.**

# Chapter 5
# Tethered Fates

The world came back in fragments—blurry edges, muted sounds, and a sharp ache pulsing at the base of Selene's skull. She gasped, her lungs burning as if she'd been underwater too long. When she opened her eyes, the familiar, dim outline of her apartment greeted her. The ceiling's cracked plaster, the faint hum of the city beyond her window, and the cold, unforgiving light slipping through half-closed blinds. But something was wrong.

Her body felt heavy, her mind still tangled with echoes of the voices that had haunted her before she collapsed. Slowly, she pushed herself upright on the couch, wincing as every muscle protested.

Then she saw it—lying on the coffee table, her hidden contract, half-unfolded, the parchment brittle and curling at the edges. The sigil in the corner, once sharp and vibrant, was now little more than a faint shadow of its former self, thin lines barely visible, like the ghost of something that had been important once.

She reached for it with trembling fingers, her breath shallow. **Almost gone.**

Before she could process it, the door creaked open. Selene's instincts kicked in—her hand darted toward the pistol tucked under the couch cushion, her body tensing for a fight.

But it wasn't a threat. Not exactly.

**Adrian Blackthorn** stepped into the room like he belonged there, like no time had passed between them. His presence filled the space, casual and intrusive, as if he hadn't carved his absence into her life years ago. His dark coat was damp from the rain outside, his sharp features shadowed by the dim light, but his eyes—those storm-gray eyes—found her instantly.

Selene didn't lower her hand from the gun.

"How the hell did you get in here?" she rasped, her voice rough with disuse.

Adrian shrugged, that infuriating, easy confidence lingering in the curve of his mouth. "You used to leave a key under the loose floorboard. Old habits, I guess."

Selene's finger twitched on the trigger. "Try another habit, like knocking."

Adrian's smirk faded slightly. He stepped further into the room, his gaze flickering to the contract on the table. His jaw tightened.

"You're not looking well, Selene."

"Gee, I wonder why," she snapped, finally lowering the gun but not putting it away. "Maybe because I've been seeing things that shouldn't exist and collapsing in alleys."

Adrian's eyes darkened. "That's why I'm here."

Selene barked a dry laugh. "You always had perfect timing. Right when the world's falling apart."

"I'm trying to protect you."

She stood abruptly, her dizziness barely noticeable under the surge of anger. "Bullshit. You don't show up to protect people. You show up when it's convenient for you—or when you've got something to hide."

Adrian flinched, just slightly, but she caught it.

"What do you know about this?" She jabbed a finger toward the contract. "About what's happening to me?"

He hesitated. That was enough of an answer.

Selene's heart pounded. "You knew."

"It's complicated," he muttered.

"No. It's not," she snapped, stepping closer. "People are dead. Their contracts torn apart, their lives—**literally**—unraveled. And now this." She held up the parchment, shaking it slightly. "This is happening to me. So stop dancing around it and tell me the truth."

Adrian rubbed the back of his neck, his confidence cracking just enough for her to see the weight he carried underneath.

"The contracts," he began slowly, "were never meant to last. They're not just agreements—they're bindings, tethers to something older than the Council, older than us."

Selene's stomach twisted. "Tethers to what?"

He met her gaze, and for the first time, she saw real fear in his eyes.

"To something that feeds on connection. On us. The Council didn't create the system—they just figured out how to exploit it."

Selene sank back onto the couch, the words settling over her like ash. "So what happens when the sigil fades completely?"

Adrian didn't answer right away. He just stared at the parchment, his expression tight.

Finally, he said, "You disappear."

Selene's throat tightened. She gripped the contract like it could anchor her to the room, to herself.

"I'm not going to disappear," she whispered, more to herself than him.

Adrian stepped closer, his voice softer now. "That's why I'm here. I can help you. But you have to trust me."

She let out a bitter laugh. "Trust? You think you've earned that?"

"I know I haven't," he said quietly. "But I'm all you've got."

Selene looked at him, really looked—at the man who'd once been her anchor, now a stranger wrapped in familiar skin. The ache in her chest wasn't from fear. It was from memory.

She didn't know if she could trust him.

But she didn't have many choices left.

--------

The tension in the room was a living thing, thick and suffocating, coiling around Selene's chest like it wanted to squeeze the air out of her lungs. She stood by the cracked window, the faint city lights casting fractured shadows across the walls. Adrian lingered near the door, arms crossed, his posture casual but his eyes sharp, stormy with something unspoken.

Selene's fingers tightened around the faded contract, its fragile edges crumpling slightly under the pressure. She didn't care. It felt like the only real thing left in the room.

"So," she said, breaking the heavy silence, her voice low and cold. "You've been working with the Council."

Adrian didn't flinch. "It's not that simple."

"Oh, it's *exactly* that simple." She spun around to face him, the anger bubbling just beneath the surface. "You show up out of nowhere, spouting half-truths, acting like you're here to 'protect me,' and now I find out you've been in bed with the same people pulling the strings?"

Adrian's jaw tightened. "I didn't have a choice."

"There's always a choice," she snapped, taking a step closer. "You just made the one that kept you safe."

His eyes darkened, and for a moment, the mask slipped. "You think I'm safe? You think working for them hasn't cost me anything?"

Selene laughed, bitter and sharp. "Oh, please. Spare me the martyr routine."

Adrian closed the distance between them in two quick strides, his voice low and rough. "You have no idea what I've done to keep you out of this."

She glared at him, her chest rising and falling with shallow breaths. "I never asked you to."

"No," he whispered, softer now, "but I did it anyway."

The words hung between them, heavy with everything they weren't saying.

Selene looked away first, her gaze dropping to the contract in her hands. The sigil was nearly gone, just faint lines fading into nothing.

"What do you want from me, Adrian?"

His voice was quieter when he answered, but no less intense. "I want you to survive."

She shook her head, frustration knotting in her chest. "Why? So I can be another puppet in their game?"

Adrian's expression softened, and that was worse than the anger. "Because you're the key to stopping this."

Selene froze, her heart skipping. "What are you talking about?"

He stepped back, running a hand through his hair, pacing now like he couldn't stand still. "The contracts—they're failing. The bindings are unraveling, and when they collapse completely, it won't just be the people connected to them who suffer. It'll be *everyone*."

Selene's grip tightened on the parchment. "And you think I can fix it?"

Adrian stopped, meeting her eyes with a look that was part desperation, part hope. "I don't just think it. I know it."

She swallowed hard, the weight of his words settling over her like lead.

"And if I say no?" she whispered.

Adrian's jaw clenched. "Then we all burn."

Selene stared at him, her mind racing, her heart pounding like it wanted to escape her chest. She wanted to scream, to throw something, to push him away and pretend none of this was real.

But it was.

And deep down, she knew he was right.

She just didn't know if she could forgive him for it.

--------

The apartment felt too small for both of them, the walls pressing inward, filled with echoes of old arguments and the ghosts of things left unsaid. Selene paced, her fingers twitching against the frayed edge of her sleeve, while Adrian stood near the window, his silhouette framed by the dim city lights bleeding through the blinds.

"We don't have time to fight about this," Adrian said finally, breaking the tense silence.

Selene shot him a sharp look. "No, we don't. But we seem to have time for you to lie."

Adrian exhaled, rubbing the back of his neck. "I didn't lie."

"Lies of omission count," she snapped. "Especially when people's lives are on the line."

His jaw tightened. "I did what I had to."

"And now you need me to clean up the mess," she shot back, her voice low, sharp as a blade. "Typical."

Adrian stepped forward, his expression darkening. "You think this is just my mess? You think the Council's games only revolve around me?"

Selene stopped pacing, turning to face him fully. "No. But you're the common thread."

Adrian's lips pressed into a thin line. "So are you."

That hit harder than she wanted to admit. She clenched her fists, trying to ignore the faint tremor in her hands. The sigil wasn't just fading; it felt like it was taking pieces of her with it.

She swallowed hard, her voice quieter when she spoke again. "What's in the Black Library?"

Adrian hesitated, then said, "Everything the Council doesn't want anyone to know. The origin of the contracts. The binding rituals. How to break them."

Selene's heart raced. "You think the answer's there?"

"I know it is," he said. "But it's not just about finding answers. It's about surviving long enough to use them."

Selene stared at him, her mind racing. She hated this—hated needing him, hated that his name was tied to every thread she pulled. But the truth was undeniable: she couldn't do this alone.

"Fine," she muttered. "We do this together. But this is a fragile alliance. You step out of line, and I swear—"

Adrian raised a brow. "You'll shoot me?"

Selene's glare was answer enough.

He smirked slightly, but it faded as quickly as it appeared. "I'll take my chances."

She moved to the small table, shoving aside old files to make space. "So, how do we get in?"

Adrian leaned against the wall, crossing his arms. "The Black Library isn't just a building. It's buried beneath the Council's archives, hidden under layers of security—magical and otherwise."

"Of course it is," Selene muttered, dragging a hand through her hair. "And you have a plan?"

"I have a start," Adrian corrected. "There's someone who can get us through the first barrier. After that..." He shrugged.

"Improvisation. Great," Selene said dryly. She grabbed a pen, scribbling notes on the back of an old receipt. "When do we leave?"

Adrian's gaze drifted to the faded contract still sitting on the table. "Soon. The sigil's almost gone."

Selene followed his gaze, her chest tightening. She could feel it slipping away—not just the contract, but something inside her. Like threads unraveling, one by one.

"We don't have a choice," she whispered, more to herself than him.

Adrian's voice was soft when he replied. "We never did."

She didn't look at him. She couldn't. Not yet.

But she didn't stop him from staying.

# Chapter 6
# The Black Library

The night clung to Nightrift like a second skin, thick and oppressive, smothering even the distant hum of the city. Selene and Adrian moved through its shadows, slipping past the outer defenses of the Council's archive with practiced precision. The Black Library wasn't marked on any map, not even within the Council's own records. It existed beneath the façade of bureaucratic offices—a secret buried under layers of stone, magic, and lies.

Selene's heart thudded with a steady, measured rhythm as she pressed herself against the cold wall, peering around the corner. Two guards stood near a heavy iron door, their uniforms crisp, but their postures bored. She glanced at Adrian, whose expression was a mask of calm, though she could see the tension lurking beneath.

"You take the one on the left," she whispered.

Adrian arched a brow. "I thought I was the distraction."

Selene smirked faintly. "You are. Just make sure you're distracting enough."

Without waiting for a reply, she moved.

Selene was a shadow, swift and silent, her blade flashing briefly under the dim emergency lights. One guard went down without a sound, her grip firm as she eased his body to the floor. Across from her, Adrian handled the other with brutal efficiency—a sharp twist, a muffled gasp, and then silence.

They exchanged a glance. No words were needed.

The door was the real problem. It wasn't just locked; it was sealed with layers of protective enchantments, the faint glow of runes etched into the metal like veins pulsing under skin. Selene's breath fogged in the suddenly cold air.

Adrian stepped forward, his fingers brushing over the sigils. His face tightened with concentration.

"This isn't just a lock," he murmured. "It's a ward. Old magic. Designed to keep things in as much as out."

Selene's fingers twitched toward her sidearm out of habit, though she knew bullets wouldn't do much against ancient magic. "Can you break it?"

Adrian didn't answer immediately. His eyes darkened, shadows flickering across his face as he muttered something under his breath. The runes flared, pulsed once—and then dimmed.

The door creaked open.

"Lucky guess," he said, though his voice lacked its usual charm.

Selene didn't reply. She stepped into the darkness beyond, her flashlight slicing through the gloom. The Black Library was nothing like she'd expected. It wasn't a sterile archive of neatly labeled files. It was a labyrinth, carved deep into the earth, its walls lined with shelves crammed full of ancient tomes bound in leather, metal, and—she didn't want to think about what else.

The air was thick, heavy with dust and something darker—an invisible pressure that made her skin crawl. It wasn't just old. It was alive. She could feel it pulsing, like the library itself was breathing, its walls watching.

"This place feels wrong," she muttered.

Adrian's eyes flicked around, sharp and wary. "Because it *is* wrong. The Council doesn't keep knowledge here. They keep it *trapped.*"

They moved deeper, the narrow corridors twisting in impossible ways. Selene marked their path with chalk on the walls, though she had the nagging sense the marks wouldn't be there if they turned back.

Suddenly, Adrian froze, his hand shooting out to stop her.

"Trap," he whispered, pointing to a faint shimmer on the floor. A rune, almost invisible, etched into the stone.

Selene crouched, examining it. "Can you disarm it?"

Adrian hesitated, then shook his head. "I can try. But if I'm wrong…"

Selene stood, drawing her blade. "Then let's not find out."

With careful precision, they found a narrow ledge along the wall, barely wide enough to balance on. Selene led the way, her breath shallow as she edged past the trap. Adrian followed, his movements silent despite the tension radiating off him.

Once past, Selene exhaled slowly. "This better be worth it."

Adrian gave a wry smile. "Isn't it always?"

They continued, the oppressive weight of the library growing with every step. The air felt thicker, the darkness deeper. Selene could feel her pulse in her fingertips, in her throat. The sigil on her contract, tucked safely in her coat, pulsed faintly against her skin, like it was reacting to the place.

Or to something waiting within it.

Finally, they reached a massive door, unlike the others. This one wasn't sealed with runes or locks. It simply stood closed, as if daring them to open it.

Adrian hesitated. "This is it."

Selene nodded, her hand resting on the door.

She didn't know what waited beyond. But she knew one thing—**there was no turning back.**

---

The heavy door groaned as Selene pushed it open, its rusted hinges protesting against years of disuse. A rush of cold, stale air met them, carrying the scent of old parchment, damp stone, and something metallic—like blood left too long on steel. The room beyond was vast, dimly lit by flickering lanterns suspended from chains, their flames unnaturally steady despite the absence of wind.

Rows upon rows of shelves stretched into the darkness, crammed with ancient tomes, scrolls sealed with crumbling wax, and relics that hummed faintly with residual magic. The oppressive silence settled over them like a suffocating blanket, broken only by the soft echo of their footsteps against the cold stone floor.

Adrian's voice was low, his breath misting slightly in the frigid air. "This is it. The heart of the Black Library."

Selene didn't respond, her eyes scanning the shelves, searching for something—anything—that would make sense of the chaos unraveling in her life. She moved with purpose, her fingers trailing along spines etched with symbols older than any language she recognized.

"Whatever we're looking for," she muttered, "it's here."

Adrian followed, his expression tense. "The Council didn't just build this place to hide knowledge. They built it to contain it."

Selene shot him a glance. "Contain what?"

He didn't answer.

After minutes of searching, she found a large, leather-bound book tucked into the corner of a dusty shelf. The cover was cracked, embossed with an unfamiliar sigil that made her skin crawl just looking at it. She pulled it free, the weight of it heavier than expected, and laid it on a nearby table.

Adrian peered over her shoulder as she flipped through brittle pages filled with spidery handwriting and crude diagrams. Symbols, contracts, names written and crossed out with meticulous precision. But it was the illustration near the middle that made her freeze—a detailed sketch of figures shrouded in darkness, tendrils extending from them, threading into the hearts of human silhouettes.

Selene's stomach turned. "What the hell is this?"

Adrian's face had gone pale. "The Veilborn."

She frowned. "Veilborn?"

He nodded slowly, his voice barely above a whisper. "Entities from beyond the Veil. Not gods. Not demons. Something… older. They don't live. They *exist*, and they hunger for one thing."

Selene's fingers tightened on the pages. "Souls."

Adrian swallowed hard. "The contracts—they're not about unity. They were never about love, or legal bonds. They're transactions. The sigils aren't marks of commitment. They're seals. Binding souls as currency."

Selene's breath hitched, her mind racing to the faded contract tucked in her coat. The missing sigils from the crime scenes. The twisted bodies. It all clicked into place like shards of broken glass.

"So every person bound by a contract…"

Adrian finished for her, his voice hollow. "Is a vessel. A tether to feed the Veilborn."

Selene slammed the book shut, her hands shaking. "And the Council?"

"They're not just aware of it," Adrian said bitterly. "They're the brokers. The middlemen in a deal struck long before we were even born."

Selene stepped back, her pulse pounding in her ears. "How long have you known?"

Adrian hesitated, then met her gaze. "Long enough."

Her anger flared, sharp and immediate. "And you said nothing."

"What would you have done if I had?" he shot back. "Run straight into their arms? Challenged them without knowing what you were up against?"

"I'm doing that now!"

Adrian's face twisted with frustration. "Because you're already in too deep."

Selene turned away, her fists clenched. She felt the pull of the contract against her skin, the faint, dying pulse of the sigil like a heartbeat that wasn't hers.

"This isn't just about me," she whispered. "It's about *everyone*."

Adrian stepped closer, his voice softer now. "I know."

She closed her eyes, drawing in a shaky breath. When she opened them, she was steady again—fueled by purpose, if not clarity.

"Then we find a way to break the deal."

Adrian's smile was faint, tinged with something like admiration—or regret. "That's the problem with deals like this, Selene."

She met his gaze, fire burning behind her eyes. "They can be broken."

---

The narrow halls of the Black Library seemed to pulse with a life of their own as Selene and Adrian sprinted through the labyrinth of ancient shelves and crumbling relics. The stolen tome was clutched tightly in Selene's hand, its weight both literal and metaphorical—a book that held the truth about the contracts, the Veilborn, and the Council's darkest secrets.

Every flickering lantern they passed seemed to dim in their wake, as if the very shadows were trying to swallow them whole.

Selene's breath was ragged, her pulse pounding in her ears, but she didn't slow. She could feel it—**something** was coming. The walls seemed to narrow, the oppressive energy thickening like fog. They rounded a corner, and there he stood.

A **Council enforcer**, clad in dark robes etched with crimson sigils that glimmered faintly under the sickly light. His face was obscured by a mask, featureless except for a single black line running vertically down the center. But it wasn't his appearance that made Selene's heart stutter—it was the power radiating off him, like standing too close to a raging fire.

Adrian skidded to a halt beside her, his breath hitching. "Damn it."

The enforcer stepped forward, his voice a low, distorted whisper that seemed to echo from everywhere at once. "You shouldn't be here."

Selene didn't wait for an invitation. She raised her gun and fired.

The bullet stopped mid-air, suspended as if caught in invisible fingers. The enforcer flicked his wrist, and the round reversed course, slicing past Selene's cheek with a hiss of heat before embedding itself in the wall behind her.

Adrian reacted fast, his hand darting out, muttering a sharp incantation under his breath. A burst of kinetic energy shot toward the enforcer, but it dissipated on impact, like water against stone.

The enforcer lifted his hand, and darkness surged forward—a tendril of shadow shaped like a spear.

Selene dove to the side, rolling behind a pillar, her heart hammering. She peeked out to see Adrian already on the offensive, summoning a blade of pure energy, its edges flickering like fire. He lunged, the blade meeting the enforcer's conjured weapon in a clash that sent shockwaves rippling through the room.

Selene didn't hesitate. She moved fast, flanking the enforcer, firing again. This time the bullet grazed his shoulder, tearing through the fabric. He barely flinched.

The enforcer spun, his hand snapping out, and a surge of dark magic slammed into Selene like a freight train. She was thrown backward, crashing against a shelf that collapsed under the impact, ancient books and debris raining down around her.

Pain flared, but something else—*worse*—ignited in her chest.

Her sigil.

It burned like a brand pressed to her skin, searing hot, the edges of her vision blurring with light and shadow. She gasped, clutching her side, feeling the faint pulse of something vast and ancient **not just watching her—but reaching for her.**

The Veilborn knew.

Adrian roared in defiance, pushing himself harder, his strikes growing wild, desperate. He landed a blow—a deep gash across the enforcer's chest—but it came at a cost. The enforcer retaliated with a blast of dark energy, slamming into Adrian's side with brutal force.

Adrian crumpled to the ground, blood blooming dark against his shirt.

"No!" Selene's scream was raw, cutting through the chaos.

She pushed past the pain, dragging herself up, her hands trembling as she raised her gun again. But it wasn't the weapon that saved her.

It was the sigil.

With a final, blinding surge of pain, it flared—*not fading this time, but burning bright*—and the force of it erupted from her in a shockwave of raw, untamed energy. The enforcer was thrown back, crashing into the far wall with enough force to leave a crater in the stone.

Selene collapsed beside Adrian, her hands shaking as she pressed against his wound, trying to stem the bleeding.

"Stay with me," she whispered, her voice thick with fear she didn't have time to process.

Adrian coughed, blood staining his lips. "You've… got one hell of a temper."

Selene choked out a broken laugh, tears burning in her eyes. "Shut up. You're not dying. Not here."

She didn't know how she'd get them out. She didn't know what was happening to her.

But she knew one thing—the Veilborn had found her.

And this was only the beginning.

# Chapter 7
# Fractured Truths

The safehouse was buried beneath the city, hidden within the skeleton of an old subway station long since forgotten. Crumbling tiles lined the walls, and the faint scent of rust and damp concrete lingered in the air. A single flickering bulb cast long shadows across the narrow space, its dim glow illuminating a battered metal cot where **Adrian** lay, his face pale and slick with sweat. His breathing was shallow, uneven—every exhale a painful reminder of how close she'd come to losing him.

**Selene** sat beside him, her hands stained with dried blood, the ragged edges of her resolve fraying more with each hour that passed. She wasn't a medic. She'd seen plenty of wounds in her time, patched up more than she cared to admit—but this was different. The injury from the enforcer's dark magic wasn't just physical. It was something deeper, something that seemed to pull at Adrian's very essence, like his soul was fraying at the edges.

The makeshift bandages were soaked through, the crimson stark against his skin. She pressed down harder, trying to staunch the bleeding, ignoring his weak groan of protest.

"Don't you dare," she muttered under her breath, voice tight with fear she refused to show. "You don't get to die on me."

Adrian's eyelids fluttered, his breath hitching as he forced his eyes open. They were clouded, unfocused, but there was still a spark of recognition when they met hers.

"Your bedside manner... needs work," he rasped, his voice little more than a whisper.

Selene exhaled sharply, not sure if it was relief or frustration. Probably both. "Shut up and stay still."

A weak smile tugged at the corner of his mouth, but it faded quickly as pain etched lines across his face. He winced, his hand trembling as he reached for her wrist.

"Selene," he breathed, his grip weak but insistent. "The sigil... it's connected. You feel it too, don't you?"

She hesitated, her fingers pausing over the wound. The memory of that searing pain, the blinding flare of her sigil in the Black Library—it haunted her like an echo she couldn't escape. It wasn't just a mark anymore. It was something alive, something ancient, tangled in her veins.

"I feel it," she admitted quietly, not meeting his gaze. "But right now, I'm more concerned with you *not* bleeding out on this damn floor."

He tried to laugh, but it turned into a cough, blood speckling his lips. She swore under her breath, grabbing a cloth to wipe it away.

"You should've left me," he murmured, his voice growing fainter.

Selene froze, her jaw tightening. "That's not who I am."

Adrian's eyes fluttered shut again, his breathing ragged. Panic surged in her chest, cold and sharp, but she forced it down, focusing on the rhythm of the tasks—apply pressure, check for signs of infection, keep him warm. *Keep him alive.*

Hours bled into one another, the only sounds the distant drip of water from a cracked pipe and Adrian's labored breaths. Selene didn't sleep. She couldn't. Instead, she sat vigil, her mind spiraling through memories she'd tried to bury.

His laugh, soft and warm on quiet mornings. The way he used to look at her like she was the only person in the room. And then—the day he walked away, his back disappearing into the crowd, leaving her with nothing but questions and anger.

She shook the thoughts away, focusing on the present. On the man barely clinging to life in front of her.

When his fever finally broke, it felt like the tension in her chest eased just enough for her to breathe.

Adrian's eyes opened slowly, clearer this time, though exhaustion still weighed heavy on him. He looked at her for a long moment, as if trying to figure out if she was real.

"You stayed," he whispered, voice rough and weak.

Selene didn't look away. "Yeah," she said softly. "I stayed."

For once, there was no bitterness in her voice. Just truth.

Because despite everything—the lies, the betrayals, the fractured past—they were still here.

And maybe that meant something.

--------

The safehouse was quieter now, though the silence wasn't comforting. It had a brittle quality, like glass on the verge of shattering. **Adrian** was asleep on the cot, his breathing still uneven but steady enough that Selene finally allowed herself to step away. She didn't go far. She never did.

Across the room, under the flickering light of an ancient bulb, **Elias Gray** hunched over the stolen tome, his fingers tracing faded ink and cracked parchment with an almost reverent caution. His workspace was a chaotic sprawl of notes, sketches, and symbols that Selene couldn't begin to understand. The faint scent of burnt sage lingered, mixed with old paper and ink—a sharp contrast to the metallic tang of dried blood that still clung to her memory.

Selene leaned against the doorframe, arms crossed, her gaze sharp despite the exhaustion dragging at her bones.

"Well?" she asked, her voice cutting through the silence.

Elias didn't look up. "Impatient as ever."

"I don't have the luxury of patience."

With a sigh, Elias closed the book, his fingers steepling under his chin. His face was drawn, shadows clinging to the hollows beneath his eyes.

"You were right about one thing," he began quietly. "The contracts aren't just legal bindings. They're something older, woven with magic that predates the Council itself. They tether not just people to each other but to the Veil—the space between life and death."

Selene's jaw tightened. "Tell me something I don't know."

Elias's eyes flicked to her then, sharp and unflinching. "Breaking a contract isn't as simple as tearing it apart. There's a balance to be maintained. A debt."

"A debt?" Selene pushed off the wall, her heart pounding.

"Blood," Elias confirmed. "The contracts are bound by life essence. When you break that bond, something—or someone—has to pay the price."

Selene felt the words settle in her chest like a stone. "So what? Every person who's had their contract broken…"

"They didn't just die," Elias said softly. "They were the payment."

A cold chill swept over her, the memory of twisted bodies and hollowed eyes flashing behind her eyelids.

She swallowed hard. "And if it's my contract?"

Elias hesitated, his gaze dropping to the parchment spread before him. "Yours is different. It's not just a contract—it's an anchor. A conduit."

"For what?"

"For *them*," he whispered. "The Veilborn."

Selene's throat went dry. She'd heard the name before, but now it felt heavier, like it carried weight beyond language.

"So if I break it—" She couldn't finish the sentence.

Elias met her gaze, his expression grim. "It won't just be your life. The cost could ripple beyond you. The Veil doesn't like unpaid debts. It'll take what it's owed."

Selene's breath hitched. She glanced toward Adrian, his face pale against the stained pillow.

"What if I don't break it?" she asked quietly.

Elias didn't answer right away. When he did, his voice was softer, almost kind. "Then it'll break *you*."

Silence settled between them, thick and suffocating. Selene stared at the floor, her mind racing.

"So I'm screwed either way," she muttered, more to herself than Elias.

He didn't argue.

Selene turned, retreating back to Adrian's side, her hand brushing against the faint pulse of the fading sigil beneath her collarbone. It burned like a quiet promise, a reminder of the inevitable.

But she wasn't ready to accept that.

Not yet.

---

The safehouse grew colder with each passing hour, though there was no logical reason for it. The air felt heavier, pressing against Selene's chest like invisible hands, making it hard to breathe. The walls seemed closer than before, shadows pooling in the corners, stretching longer than they should. She tried to ignore it, to focus on Adrian's recovery and Elias's grim research, but something was shifting inside her—a fracture growing deeper with every heartbeat.

She didn't sleep anymore. Couldn't.

The first vision crept in when she was alone, her back against the cold brick wall, fingers unconsciously tracing the fading lines of her sigil beneath her collarbone. The edges of the room blurred, the flickering bulb above her dimming into darkness until only the faint outline of the door remained.

Then she heard it—a whisper, faint and layered, like voices speaking over one another in a language she didn't understand.

*Selene...*

Her head snapped up, heart pounding. The room was empty. Adrian still slept, his shallow breaths the only sound anchoring her to reality. But the shadows weren't still anymore. They shifted, sliding along the walls with an unnatural grace, coiling like smoke.

She forced herself to her feet, fists clenched, every instinct screaming that something was wrong. "Who's there?"

Silence answered first.

Then the shadows peeled away from the corners, gathering into the vague shape of a figure. No face, no eyes—just darkness wrapped in the suggestion of human form.

*"You're unraveling,"* it whispered, the words slithering into her mind rather than her ears. *"But you don't have to."*

Selene's pulse roared in her ears. She reached for her gun out of habit, but her fingers met empty air. She wasn't sure when it had vanished—or if it ever existed in this space. The walls were gone now, replaced by endless blackness, the ground beneath her feet feeling insubstantial, as if she could fall through at any moment.

"What do you want?" she rasped, her voice sounding too small.

*"Not what we want,"* the figure replied, its form rippling like disturbed water. *"What we offer."*

The darkness shifted again, and suddenly she wasn't in the safehouse anymore. She was standing in the Black Library's ruins, the air thick with ash and the stench of blood. Adrian lay on the ground at her feet, lifeless, his eyes glassy and empty. Her heart lurched, and she dropped to her knees beside him, trying to shake him awake—but her hands passed through him like smoke.

*"You can save him,"* the voice hissed, closer now, wrapping around her like a serpent. *"You can save them all. Just say yes."*

Selene squeezed her eyes shut, her nails digging into her palms. *This isn't real. This isn't real.*

But the pain felt real.

The grief felt real.

She forced herself to stand, shaking with rage and fear. "I'm not yours," she growled.

The shadows laughed—a hollow, empty sound. *"Not yet."*

She woke on the floor, drenched in sweat, her body trembling, muscles aching like she'd been fighting something for hours. Elias hovered over her, his face a mask of worry and something else—fear.

"What happened?" she croaked, her throat raw.

"You were out for hours," he said, helping her sit up. "Seizing."

Selene pressed a trembling hand to her chest. The sigil burned like fire, brighter than before, pulsing in rhythm with her heart.

"They're inside me," she whispered, more to herself than Elias. "The Veilborn. They're in."

Elias didn't argue.

Because it was the truth.

The visions didn't stop after that. They came when she was awake, when she blinked too long, when the shadows grew too deep. Each time, they whispered her name, promised her power, salvation, control.

*"You don't have to be afraid,"* they'd say. *"Let go."*

But she didn't.

She wouldn't.

Even as it tore her apart from the inside out.

# Chapter 8
# The Tether's Price

The safehouse felt smaller now, suffocating with every breath Selene took. The cracked walls seemed to close in, their jagged shadows stretched thin under the dim glow of the single flickering bulb overhead. The news had arrived with the subtlety of a dagger slipped between the ribs—delivered not with force, but precision.

The warrant wasn't just a piece of paper. It was a declaration, etched in cold, bureaucratic ink.

**Selene Ward:Wanted for treason against the Council. Charges: Espionage, conspiracy, unauthorized use of restricted artifacts, and obstruction of justice. Shoot on sight if necessary.**

She read it again, her fingers gripping the crumpled paper as if she could squeeze the words into oblivion. The Council's seal was stamped at the bottom, bold and final, like an executioner's signature.

"They're serious," Elias muttered from across the room, his voice laced with something between amusement and pity. "Treason, huh? That's impressive even for you."

Selene shot him a glare sharp enough to cut glass. "I'm glad my impending death is so entertaining."

Adrian sat nearby, his recovery still visible in the way he moved—stiff, deliberate, his wounds stitched with makeshift supplies and stubbornness. He didn't say anything, his gaze dark as he stared at the warrant.

Selene crumpled the paper into a tight fist and tossed it onto the floor. "It was only a matter of time."

Adrian finally spoke, his voice low. "It's not just a warrant. It's a message."

Selene nodded, pacing. "They're forcing my hand. Either I run, or I die. No middle ground."

Elias leaned back in his chair, crossing his arms. "What about your friends in the precinct? Mendez?"

Selene froze mid-step. The thought of **Mendez**—his easy grin, his sharp instincts—sent a pang through her chest. She'd trusted him with cases, with her life more than once. But this wasn't just a case. This was a war, and she wasn't sure which side he'd choose.

Adrian seemed to read her hesitation. "You think he'll turn on you?"

She didn't answer right away. "I think he'll do what he thinks is right."

"That's not the same thing."

No, it wasn't.

Later, under the cover of darkness, Selene made her way to an abandoned warehouse near the waterfront—a place she knew Mendez used when he needed space away from the precinct's watchful eyes. She found him there, leaning against his car, his face shadowed but unmistakable.

He saw her before she fully stepped into view, his hand hovering near his sidearm.

"Mendez," she called softly, raising her hands to show she wasn't armed.

His jaw tightened. "You shouldn't be here."

"I know."

A heavy silence stretched between them, filled only by the distant sounds of waves lapping against the dock.

"They put out a warrant," he said, his voice flat.

"I've seen it."

Mendez shifted, his eyes scanning the darkness behind her. "They say you're working against the Council. That you've… changed."

Selene felt a bitter laugh rise, but she swallowed it. "They're right about one thing. I'm not the same."

"Why?" His voice cracked slightly, frustration bleeding through. "Why didn't you come to me sooner? I could've—"

"Could've what?" she snapped, stepping closer. "Protected me? Covered for me? This isn't about bending the rules, Mendez. The Council isn't just corrupt—they're feeding on people, using contracts to bind souls. You think I'm the bad guy because I won't play along?"

His hand dropped from his holster, fingers curling into a fist. "I don't know what to think."

Selene's breath hitched. "Then *don't* think. Just listen. I didn't kill anyone. I didn't betray the city. But if we don't stop them, there won't be anything left to protect."

Mendez's face hardened, the lines of conflict etched deep. "Do you even hear yourself? Contracts? Souls? That's not the Selene I know."

"No," she whispered. "It's not."

A long pause.

Then, slowly, Mendez pulled a small envelope from his jacket, tossing it toward her. She caught it, fingers trembling slightly.

"What's this?"

"Information," he muttered. "Files I pulled from the precinct. I don't know why, but… I think you'll need them."

Selene stared at him, her chest tight. "You believe me?"

Mendez didn't answer. He just turned, walking back to his car.

As the engine roared to life, he called over his shoulder, "Don't make me regret this."

She watched him drive away, her heart heavier than when she'd arrived.

Back at the safehouse, Selene sat in silence, staring at the envelope in her hands.

Mendez had made his choice.

Now, it was her turn.

--------

The road stretched out before them, winding through the outskirts of Nightrift where the city's suffocating grip loosened, giving way to forgotten places. The world felt quieter here, but it was the kind of quiet that pressed into your ears, heavy with the weight of things left unsaid. **Selene** sat in the passenger seat of a battered, unregistered vehicle Adrian had managed to procure, her fingers tracing the faint, faded sigil beneath the collar of her shirt. It pulsed faintly, like an ember refusing to die.

Adrian drove in silence, his face set in that familiar, unreadable mask she'd come to resent. His injuries had mostly healed, though a faint stiffness lingered in the way he gripped the wheel, his knuckles white against the cracked leather. They didn't talk much anymore. Words felt fragile, and neither of them could afford to break under the weight of their truths.

The destination was an abandoned industrial complex hidden in the shadow of the old railway lines, where the Council's influence was little more than a whisper. This was where the **Revenants**—ancient rebels who had fought against the Council's grip long before Selene was even born—had gone to disappear. The kind of people who didn't just live in the shadows; they *became* them.

They stepped out of the car, the cold night air biting against Selene's skin. She scanned the decaying buildings, their walls tagged with faded symbols, remnants of forgotten rebellions. Adrian led the way through rusted gates and crumbling hallways, until they reached a door marked with an old sigil—one that felt strangely familiar, though Selene couldn't explain why.

Inside, the air was thick with dust and old secrets. Dim lanterns cast flickering shadows on stone walls etched with strange markings. Figures emerged from the darkness, silent and watchful. Armed, but not immediately hostile.

A woman stepped forward, her presence commanding. She was older, her face a map of scars and hard-won battles, eyes sharp as broken glass. **Maelen**—the name whispered through rebel circles like a myth. She studied Selene with a gaze that felt like it could strip flesh from bone.

"So," Maelen said, voice rough like gravel. "This is the girl who's got the Council shaking."

Selene lifted her chin. "I'm not here to impress anyone."

Maelen's lips twitched into something between a smirk and a sneer. "Good. We're not here to be impressed."

Adrian exchanged a glance with Selene before speaking. "We need answers."

Maelen gestured for them to follow deeper into the hideout. They passed relics from past wars—broken sigils, burnt parchment, weapons etched with symbols Selene didn't recognize but felt deep in her bones. They stopped in a room with a large table covered in maps, documents, and fragments of contracts older than any Council record.

"You're not just tangled up in this mess," Maelen said, leaning over the table. "You *are* the mess."

Selene frowned. "What the hell does that mean?"

Another figure, an older man named **Corvin**, stepped into the dim light, his eyes cold but calculating. "Your bloodline," he said simply. "You're tied to the original Veil contracts. The ones the Council built their empire on."

Selene's stomach dropped, the words hitting harder than any blow. "That's not possible."

Maelen's gaze didn't waver. "It's not just possible. It's fact."

Adrian stiffened beside her. "What does that make her?"

"A target," Corvin replied. "And a weapon."

Selene took a step back, her mind racing. "I didn't ask for this."

Maelen shrugged. "No one does. But it's in your blood. That sigil fading? It's not just a mark. It's a key."

"A key to what?"

"To breaking the chains—or reforging them," Corvin answered. "Depends on who gets to you first."

Selene's heart pounded, the weight of it all pressing down like a vice. She wasn't just part of the story. She *was* the story.

And there was no way to run from it now.

She looked at Adrian, his face unreadable, but she could see it in his eyes—he'd suspected. Maybe even known.

The betrayal stung, but it didn't matter anymore.

All that mattered was what came next.

--------

The darkness came without warning.

Selene had barely registered the sharp sting at the base of her skull before the world tilted, her knees buckling beneath her. Voices blurred into muffled echoes, shapes dissolving into shadows as the ground rushed up to meet her. The last thing she saw was Adrian's face—wide-eyed, reaching for her—and then everything went black.

When she woke, the cold was the first thing she felt. A biting, sterile chill that seeped into her bones. Her wrists were bound with metallic cuffs etched with faint sigils, draining whatever strength she had left. The room was stark and suffocating, all sharp edges and blinding white light that felt like it was trying to strip her down to nothing.

She wasn't alone.

Across from her, perched like vultures in seats carved from dark stone, sat the **Council**. Their robes were pristine, faces masked or half-hidden, but their presence was undeniable— **predators dressed as rulers.** The air felt heavier here, thick with invisible chains that pressed against her chest.

A figure stepped forward, his voice smooth as glass. **Councilor Thane,** the one Selene had seen only in reports, now standing like a ghost made flesh. His gaze was sharp enough to cut, though he smiled like this was all just a formality.

"Selene Ward," he began, his tone polite, almost warm. "We've been expecting you."

Selene straightened despite the weight of the cuffs, her lip curling into a defiant sneer. "Funny. I wasn't planning to RSVP."

A faint chuckle rippled through the council chamber, more chilling than amused.

Thane circled her slowly, his hands clasped behind his back. "You've caused quite the disruption. The Black Library. The stolen documents. Aligning yourself with traitors." He paused, leaning closer, his smile fading. "And yet, here you are. Alone."

Selene's jaw clenched. "I'm not the one hiding behind masks."

Thane's eyes darkened, but his smile returned, razor-thin. "You're bold. I admire that."

She didn't respond. Words were useless here.

Thane stopped in front of her, his gaze drifting to the faint, fading sigil glowing weakly beneath her collarbone. "The tether is almost gone," he murmured, more to himself than to her. "Which brings us to why you're still alive."

Selene met his gaze, her voice low and steady. "Spit it out."

Thane chuckled softly. "We're offering you a choice."

She stiffened, already knowing it wouldn't be a real choice.

"Submit," he said smoothly. "Align yourself with us. Your bloodline makes you valuable—unique. You could be more than just a detective clinging to broken ideals. You could be powerful. Immortal, even."

Selene's laugh was sharp, bitter. "Immortal? That's what this is about? Control dressed up as a gift?"

Thane's smile didn't falter. "Or you can resist," he continued, ignoring her interruption. "And be destroyed. Not just you, but everyone who stands with you. We have the power to unmake you, Selene Ward. To erase every trace you ever existed."

Her heart pounded, not with fear but fury. She leaned forward as much as her restraints allowed, her voice low and venomous. "You don't want me alive because I'm special. You want me alive because I scare you."

Silence settled over the room, sharp and suffocating.

Thane's smile faded completely. "Make your choice."

Selene closed her eyes briefly, inhaling the sterile air. She thought of Adrian, of Mendez, of the rebels who believed in something more than survival. She thought of the lives the Council had taken, the souls they'd bound, the freedom they'd stolen.

When she opened her eyes, her voice was clear and strong. "I'd rather burn than kneel."

For the first time, Thane's mask of control cracked, just a fraction.

"Then burn," he whispered.

Guards moved toward her, their steps heavy, but Selene felt something shift deep inside her—a flicker of heat where there should've been weakness. The sigil on her chest pulsed once, bright and defiant, as if her refusal had stoked a fire that even the Council couldn't control.

She wasn't gone yet.

And she wasn't going down quietly.

# Chapter 9
# Chains and Choices

The darkness in the Council's underground facility wasn't just an absence of light—it was oppressive, thick, like it had a weight of its own. The walls were slick with condensation, the faint hum of distant machinery pulsing like a heartbeat buried beneath layers of stone. Selene sat in the center of a small, windowless room, her wrists shackled above her head, metal cuffs etched with sigils designed to siphon strength, both physical and mental. The cold had seeped into her bones, but it was nothing compared to the searing pain radiating from the fading mark beneath her collarbone.

The sigil pulsed faintly, a jagged, flickering ember of what it had once been. Every throb felt like a knife twisting beneath her skin, the pain growing worse with each passing hour. She'd lost track of time—days maybe? Or hours stretched long enough to feel eternal.

The door groaned open, harsh light spilling into the room, blinding after endless darkness. **Councilor Thane** stepped in, flanked by two guards in dark uniforms. His face was the same mask of calm superiority, but there was something colder in his eyes now—an edge of frustration that he couldn't quite conceal.

"Still alive," Thane observed, his voice a smooth contrast to the harshness of the room. He approached, his steps slow and deliberate, the echo of his boots filling the silence.

Selene lifted her head with effort, her lips dry, cracked, but her glare as sharp as ever. "Disappointed?"

Thane's smile was thin. "Hardly. I'm impressed, actually. Most break long before this."

Selene's laugh was a rough rasp, more breath than sound. "Guess I'm not most people."

He circled her like a predator assessing weakened prey. "No, you're not. That's what makes this… necessary."

With a nod from Thane, one of the guards stepped forward, activating a device on the wall. Pain exploded through Selene's body—white-hot, searing, as if her very soul was being torn apart. Her back arched involuntarily, a choked scream escaping before she could stop it. The sigil on her chest flared, burning through her like wildfire, her vision blurring at the edges.

Thane watched without flinching. "The connection between you and the sigils is fascinating. It's almost poetic, really. The very thing that binds others is what's unraveling you."

Selene's breath came in ragged gasps as the pain subsided, leaving her trembling, sweat-drenched, and barely conscious. She forced a smile, blood seeping from the corner of her mouth. "You'll have to try harder."

Thane's eyes narrowed slightly, the first crack in his composed demeanor. He leaned closer, his voice dropping to a whisper.

"This isn't about breaking your body, Selene. It's about breaking *you*. Your mind, your will."

She met his gaze, her voice hoarse but steady. "You don't know me very well, then."

He straightened, adjusting his sleeves as if the conversation bored him. "We'll see."

The guard reached for the device again, but Selene's mind was already retreating inward, bracing for the next wave. This wasn't just pain—it was a war. Every scream, every shudder was a battle she refused to lose.

Between surges of agony, her thoughts flickered to Adrian, to Elias, to Mendez. To the rebellion. She couldn't be the reason they failed. Couldn't give the Council what they wanted.

As the device activated again, her vision dimmed, the edges darkening like ink bleeding through paper. But somewhere in that darkness, she felt it—a flicker of something not entirely her own.

A whisper.

*"You're stronger than this."*

It wasn't her voice.

And for the first time, she realized she wasn't entirely alone in her mind.

The sterile corridors of the Council's underground facility were carved from cold stone and steel, humming faintly with the pulse of ancient wards woven into their very foundation. Harsh fluorescent lights flickered overhead, casting long, fractured shadows. Security was tight—layers of guards, enchantments, and surveillance systems designed to be impenetrable.

But **Adrian** had never been one to follow the rules.

Dressed in the stolen uniform of a Council operative, his face hidden behind a dark mask, Adrian moved with precise, calculated steps. His heart hammered in his chest, not from fear but from the sheer gravity of what he was about to do. He'd planned every detail, mapped every hallway, but there were some things even meticulous preparation couldn't account for.

Like what it would cost him.

Reaching the security control room, he disabled the outer surveillance with swift, practiced keystrokes. The lights flickered, cameras looping on silent, empty feeds. But he knew it wouldn't hold long. The Council's systems were built to detect anomalies, and time was slipping through his fingers like sand.

He whispered under his breath, words laced with forbidden magic, tracing a sigil onto the door that led deeper into the facility. The lock hissed and clicked, the metal groaning as it gave way.

Beyond the door, Selene waited.

She was barely conscious, slumped against the cold stone wall of her cell, her wrists shackled above her head, the faint glow of her deteriorating sigil casting a weak, sickly light. Her face was bruised, blood dried along the corner of her mouth, but her spirit—Adrian could feel it—was still burning beneath the pain.

The sight of her like that ignited something fierce and raw inside him.

He moved quickly, disabling the final lock and stepping into the cell. "Selene," he whispered urgently, dropping to his knees beside her.

Her eyes fluttered open, glassy with exhaustion and pain. Recognition flickered, followed by disbelief. "Adrian?" Her voice was a rasp, strained and fragile.

"I'm here," he murmured, cupping her face gently, his thumb brushing away a streak of grime and dried blood. "I'm getting you out."

She tried to shake her head, weakly pulling against the restraints. "No… you can't… it's a trap."

Adrian's jaw tightened. "I don't care."

With trembling fingers, he traced the sigils on her cuffs. They were etched with ancient runes, designed not just to bind but to drain. He'd seen them before—used them before. But this time, breaking them meant paying a price. A steep one.

"I need to do something," he said softly, his forehead resting against hers for a brief second. "It's going to hurt."

She gave a weak smile, her eyes dark with defiance even in her weakened state. "Already hurting."

Adrian swallowed hard, then reached into his jacket, pulling out a small, obsidian shard—the **Vesper Fragment**, an artifact tied directly to the Veil. It was never meant to be used like this. But desperation had a way of rewriting rules.

He held the shard against his chest, whispering words in a language older than the Council itself. The fragment pulsed, hungry, and he felt it immediately—*the pull,* like tendrils wrapping around his soul, sinking in deep.

Agony lanced through him, sharp and blinding. His breath hitched, his knees buckling as the shard drew from him, siphoning not just his energy but something more—something essential.

A piece of his soul.

The sigils on Selene's cuffs flared, then shattered with a sound like breaking glass mixed with distant screams. She collapsed forward into his arms, her weight fragile but grounding.

Adrian's vision blurred, his strength fading fast. He cradled her face again, his breath ragged. "You're free," he whispered.

Selene's hands, shaky but determined, cupped his face. She saw the change in him immediately—the flicker of light dimmed behind his eyes, the hollowness creeping in.

"What did you do?" she rasped.

Adrian managed a weak smile. "What I should've done a long time ago."

She gripped his shirt, tears mixing with the blood on her face. "Idiot."

His laugh was a soft, broken thing. "Takes one to know one."

Footsteps echoed down the hall—guards responding to the security breach.

Selene's strength returned enough to pull him to his feet. "We're not done yet," she whispered fiercely.

Adrian nodded, though his legs barely held him. "Not even close."

Together, they stumbled toward freedom—two fractured souls bound by more than contracts, more than blood.

Bound by choice.

--------

The night air was colder than Selene remembered, sharp and biting as it filled her lungs. She stumbled through the crumbling alley, Adrian's weight pressing heavily against her as they leaned on each other for support. The Council's underground facility was far behind them now, reduced to distant echoes of alarms and the faint metallic taste of blood still lingering in her mouth.

They found refuge in the shadows of an abandoned warehouse, tucked between forgotten streets where the city's pulse couldn't reach. The space was dark, save for a single cracked window that let in slivers of moonlight, casting fractured lines across the dusty floor. Selene sank against the wall, pulling Adrian down beside her. His breathing was shallow, his face pale, the cost of their escape etched into every line of his exhausted expression.

Selene's hands trembled—not from fear but from the raw, burning ache beneath her skin. The sigil on her chest pulsed faintly, its light dim but persistent, like an ember refusing to die.

Adrian broke the silence first, his voice rough and faint. "You're alive."

Selene huffed out a bitter laugh. "So are you. Barely."

He gave a weak smile, his head resting back against the wall. "Don't sound so disappointed."

She didn't respond right away, her gaze fixed on the faint glow of her sigil. It wasn't just a mark anymore. It was a reminder—of what she'd lost, of what she'd survived, and of what she still had to do.

"I can't keep running," she whispered finally, her voice low but fierce. "I won't."

Adrian turned his head slightly, his gaze meeting hers. "Selene—"

"No," she cut him off, her jaw clenched. "They've taken everything. My life. My choices. My... soul." She laughed again, but it was hollow, brittle. "But they didn't break me."

Adrian's eyes softened. "They tried."

"And they failed."

Silence settled between them, thick with everything they didn't need to say. After a moment, Selene pushed herself up, her legs shaking but holding. She looked down at Adrian, her expression hardening with determination.

"I'm going to dismantle them," she said quietly, but her words carried the weight of a vow. "Piece by piece. Brick by brick. I'll tear down everything they've built."

Adrian's smile faded, replaced by something more serious. "It won't be easy."

She met his gaze, her sigil flickering faintly like a heartbeat. "Good."

Adrian struggled to stand, gritting his teeth against the pain. Selene reached out to steady him, her fingers lingering just a second longer than necessary.

"They'll come for us," he said softly.

She nodded. "Let them."

The faint glow of her sigil reflected in her eyes, a fragile light fueled by defiance. She was broken, yes—but not beyond repair. Not beyond rage.

As they stepped out of the shadows, the city stretched before them like a battlefield.

And Selene Ward was done running.

# Chapter 10
# War Beneath the Veil

The rebellion didn't start with a grand speech or a sweeping battle. It began in the shadows, carved out of whispered truths and stolen pages—fragments of forbidden knowledge Selene had pried from the Council's iron grip.

A flickering lantern cast fractured light across the cracked walls of the underground hideout. Maps and scattered papers littered the makeshift table, marked with notes, sigils, and red lines crisscrossing like veins. **Selene** stood at the center, her posture rigid, eyes sharp with determination, though exhaustion lingered in the tight lines around her mouth. The faint glow of the sigil on her chest pulsed steadily beneath her collar, more ember than flame now, but alive—just like her.

Around her, a small group of rebels gathered—survivors, outcasts, former Council operatives who had seen too much to stay silent. Faces she barely knew, but whose hatred for the Council burned as fiercely as her own.

Selene's gaze swept over them, her voice cutting through the low murmur like steel. "The Council built their empire on fear and control, binding us with contracts we never truly understood. They claimed it was law, but it was slavery. We're not here to beg for change. We're here to burn it all down."

A murmur of agreement rippled through the group. **Mendez** stood near the back, his arms crossed, jaw tight. Their friendship had been fractured by betrayal and secrets, but he was still here—fighting beside her. Maybe that was enough.

Adrian leaned against the wall, his face shadowed, the cost of his sacrifice still etched in the hollow beneath his eyes. He didn't speak, but Selene felt his gaze on her, steady and unyielding. It was both a comfort and a reminder of how much they had left to lose.

Selene pointed to the map spread across the table. "We've identified key Council strongholds—places where they store contracts, artifacts, and records. If we destroy them, we don't just weaken their power; we unravel it."

One of the rebels, **Kael**, a sharp-eyed former enforcer, frowned. "Even if we hit them hard, they'll retaliate. They have the Veilborn on their side."

Selene's lips curled into a cold smile. "Then we hit harder."

Kael glanced at Adrian, then back to Selene. "And what if they come for you again? You're their key. Their weapon."

Selene's hand instinctively brushed over the faint pulse of her sigil. "Let them try."

The room fell into a tense silence, broken only when Mendez stepped forward. His voice was gruff, but there was something softer beneath it—an echo of the man she used to know. "So, what's the plan?"

Selene straightened, her eyes burning with purpose. "We divide into cells. Small, fast strikes. We hit their supply lines, sabotage their networks, and expose their lies. We don't give them time to recover."

Kael nodded slowly. "Guerrilla warfare."

"Exactly."

Another rebel, **Leira**, spoke up, her voice quieter. "And when we run out of places to hide?"

Selene met her gaze without hesitation. "Then we stop hiding."

The group exchanged glances, tension mingling with grim determination. There was no illusion of victory here—just survival and vengeance, woven together like threads in the same tapestry.

Adrian finally pushed off the wall, his voice low but clear. "This isn't just about burning the Council down. It's about what comes after."

Selene turned to face him, her expression softening for the briefest moment. "We'll figure that out when we get there."

He nodded, though his eyes held a flicker of doubt she didn't have time to address.

Selene picked up one of the stolen contracts, its parchment brittle, the sigil faded. She held it up for everyone to see. "This isn't just paper. It's a chain. And we're going to break every damn one."

The rebels erupted in a chorus of agreement—raw, unpolished, but real.

As the group dispersed to prepare, Selene stood alone for a moment, the weight of leadership settling over her like a second skin. She wasn't the same detective who had stumbled onto a crime scene weeks ago. She was something else now—something forged in pain, loss, and defiance.

Her fingers brushed over her sigil one last time before she whispered to herself, "Let them come."

And when they did, she'd be ready.

--------

The rebellion surged like wildfire through the city's underbelly—swift, relentless, impossible to ignore. Explosions tore through Council archives, sacred vaults crumbled under the weight of sabotage, and for the first time in generations, the Council felt something they'd long forgotten: fear.

But with every victory, **Selene** grew weaker.

She didn't tell the others—not Adrian, not Mendez, not even Elias. They had enough to carry without the added weight of her unraveling. But it was there, gnawing at her from the inside like invisible teeth. The sigil on her chest was no longer just a faded mark. It pulsed with a faint, sickly glow, its tendrils spreading beneath her skin like cracks in glass.

She stared at herself in the cracked mirror of a dim safehouse bathroom, her reflection fragmented. Shadows crept at the edges of the glass, not reflections but **echoes**—flickering movements that shouldn't exist. Her breath came shallow, fogging the mirror slightly as the world wavered.

A whisper brushed against her ear, cold and familiar.

*"Selene…"*

She spun around, gun raised, but the room was empty.

Not real. *Not real.*

Adrian's voice pulled her back. "Selene?"

She shoved the weapon into her holster, splashing cold water on her face before stepping out. Adrian stood by the doorway, his face shadowed by concern he couldn't quite mask.

"You okay?" His gaze lingered on her face, searching for answers she wasn't ready to give.

"I'm fine," she lied smoothly, brushing past him.

He didn't follow immediately, but she felt his eyes on her back, burning with questions.

Later that night, in the flickering light of their makeshift war room, the rebellion's leaders gathered around maps scarred with red ink and hastily drawn battle plans. The hum of tension filled the air.

Mendez pointed to a marked location. "If we hit this nexus, we sever their communication lines. It'll cripple their ability to coordinate."

Selene nodded, her focus sharp despite the pounding in her skull. "We'll strike at dawn."

But as she stepped back from the table, her vision blurred. The room twisted, shadows stretching unnaturally, the voices around her fading into distant echoes. She stumbled, her hand shooting out to brace herself against the wall.

Adrian was at her side in an instant, his grip firm on her arm. "Selene."

She blinked, forcing the world back into focus. "I'm fine."

"You're not," he snapped, his voice low but fierce.

"I don't have time to—" she started, but her knees buckled, and this time, there was no catching herself.

Darkness swallowed her whole.

When she woke, the world was quieter—too quiet. She wasn't in the safehouse anymore. She was somewhere else.

The air was thick and cold, the ground beneath her a jagged black expanse that stretched into nothingness. Shadows moved without light, shifting like smoke with form and purpose. The **Veilborn** stood before her, not as fleeting whispers this time, but as towering figures made of darkness and flickering embers.

*"You cannot escape us,"* one hissed, its voice both everywhere and nowhere.

Selene clenched her fists, her breath ragged. "I'm not trying to."

The Veilborn's form rippled, its face—or what passed for one—tilting as if amused. *"You are breaking, little tether. Soon, there will be nothing left."*

She stepped forward, defiant even in this nightmare. "I'd rather break than belong to you."

*"You already do."*

Pain lanced through her chest, sharp and searing. She collapsed to her knees, gasping as the sigil burned like molten fire, its glow spreading, consuming her from the inside out.

But somewhere, faint and distant, she heard another voice—Adrian's.

"Selene! Wake up!"

She clawed at the darkness, pulling herself toward that voice, toward the fragile thread of reality. With a shuddering gasp, she opened her eyes.

Adrian hovered over her, his face etched with fear and fury. His hands gripped hers tightly, grounding her.

"You're not fine," he whispered, his voice breaking slightly.

She squeezed his hands, her own trembling. "No," she whispered back. "But I'm not gone yet."

And she wasn't. Not while there was still a fight left to win.

--------

The old train yard was a graveyard of rusted steel and forgotten memories, shrouded in mist that curled like ghostly fingers through the skeletal remains of boxcars and derelict machinery. It was the perfect place for an ambush—a trap Selene had walked into knowingly because there was no other choice. She needed to face him.

**Captain Darius Holt** stood in the center of the clearing, his figure backlit by the flickering glow of industrial floodlights, casting long shadows that seemed to stretch unnaturally around him. He looked the same as she remembered—rigid posture, sharp eyes, the weight of authority carved into every line of his face. But there was something different now, something hollow behind his gaze, as if the man she once trusted was buried beneath layers of something darker.

Selene's fingers tightened around the grip of her weapon as she stepped into the open, her breath visible in the cold night air.

"Holt," she called out, her voice cutting through the silence like a blade.

He turned slowly, his expression neutral, almost bored. "Selene Ward," he said, the familiar rasp of his voice laced with something colder—an absence where warmth used to be. "Didn't think you'd make it this far."

She smirked, masking the ache in her chest. "Yeah, well, I've always been stubborn."

He took a step forward, his hand resting casually on the holster at his hip. "You should've stayed down. You were never built for this fight."

Selene's jaw clenched. "You trained me for this fight."

A flicker of something—regret? Recognition?—passed through his eyes, but it vanished as quickly as it came. "I trained you to follow orders."

She shook her head, stepping closer. "No. You taught me to find the truth, no matter how ugly it was. That's what I'm doing now."

Holt's expression hardened. "The truth? The truth is, none of this matters. The Council is eternal. You're just another crack in the wall, and cracks get filled."

Selene's heart twisted, but she kept her voice steady. "Is that what they told you? That you're part of something bigger? Or did they just break you enough to make you believe it?"

That hit something. His face darkened, and in an instant, he drew his weapon and fired.

Selene dove behind a rusted cargo container, bullets sparking against metal. She rolled, came up firing, her shots forcing Holt to retreat into the shadows. The dance had begun—a brutal waltz of predator and prey, though Selene wasn't sure which was which anymore.

They moved through the maze of the yard, exchanging gunfire and blows, every shot and strike laced with history. Holt was fast, calculated, but Selene was fueled by something fiercer—*betrayal.*

At one point, he caught her with the butt of his rifle, sending her sprawling onto the cold ground. He was on her in a heartbeat, pinning her down, his face inches from hers.

"You never understood," he hissed, his grip tightening around her throat. "Order comes at a cost. I paid it. So will you."

Selene gasped for air, her vision blurring. But she wasn't done—not yet.

With a surge of strength, she drove her knee into his ribs, shoving him off balance. She scrambled to her feet, grabbing a metal pipe from the debris, and swung it with everything she had. It connected with a sickening crack, sending Holt sprawling.

They faced each other again, both bloodied, both breathless.

"Why?" she rasped, her voice raw with emotion. "Why did you do it?"

Holt wiped blood from his mouth, his eyes distant. "Because they showed me the truth. We're just pieces on the board. I chose to be on the winning side."

Selene's heart shattered, but there was no time to mourn. He lunged again, a knife flashing in the dim light.

This time, she was faster.

The shot rang out, echoing through the empty yard.

Holt stumbled, his eyes wide with shock as he looked down at the crimson blooming across his chest. He fell to his knees, then collapsed onto his back, staring up at the sky as if searching for something he'd never find.

Selene stood over him, her gun still trembling in her hand.

His lips moved, barely a whisper. "You… were always my best."

Tears blurred her vision, but she didn't look away. "You were supposed to be mine."

She stayed there long after his breath had stilled, the weight of the past pressing down like the darkness creeping in from the edges of the yard. The sigil on her chest flickered faintly, its glow a fragile thread tethering her to everything she'd lost—and everything she still had to fight for.

When she finally walked away, she left more than just a body behind.

She left the last piece of who she used to be.

# Chapter 11
## Crossing the Veil

The descent into the underbelly of **Nightrift** was like falling into the city's forgotten veins, where even the flicker of light seemed reluctant to linger. The ancient tunnels stretched beneath crumbling foundations, carved long before the Council claimed dominion over the living—and the dead. Every step Selene took echoed through the darkness, a fragile reminder that she was still tethered to this world, even as that connection unraveled thread by thread.

Her body was failing.

The **sigil** etched beneath her collarbone had faded to a faint shadow, its once-bright glow now little more than an ember flickering against the inevitable dark. She felt the loss in every breath, every heartbeat—a hollow ache radiating from deep within, as if her very soul was slipping away.

But her resolve had never burned brighter.

**Adrian** moved beside her, silent except for the faint scuff of his boots against the ancient stone. The tension between them was unspoken, heavy with all the things they'd never had the time—or courage—to say. His face was drawn, shadows lingering beneath his eyes from sleepless nights and the weight of sacrifices made. His hand brushed against hers once, fleeting, as if grounding himself to the fragile thread of hope they carried.

Ahead, **Elias** led the way, his lantern casting fractured light across walls etched with ancient sigils, symbols older than any Council record. The flickering flame seemed almost reluctant to touch them, as if afraid of awakening something buried too deep.

"This is it," Elias murmured, his voice reverberating off the stone like a ghost's whisper.

They stood before a massive arch carved directly into the rock, its surface covered in intricate runes that pulsed faintly—*alive,* though no magic Selene knew could explain it. The **Veil Gate.** Not just a door, but a wound in reality, stitched together with power stolen from countless souls.

Selene's knees buckled slightly, and Adrian was there instantly, his arm sliding around her waist to steady her.

"I'm fine," she rasped, though her body betrayed the lie with a violent shiver.

Adrian's jaw tightened, but he didn't argue. His grip lingered, as if letting go might break them both.

Elias approached the gate, tracing the symbols with careful fingers. "This portal predates the Council. It connects directly to the **source**—the heart of the Veil, where the contracts draw their power. If you confront it there, you can sever the tether."

Selene forced herself upright, every muscle screaming in protest. "And if I fail?"

Elias glanced over his shoulder, his expression grim. "Then there won't be enough left of you to regret it."

The words settled over them like ash.

Selene stepped forward, her hand trembling as she pressed it against the cold stone. The runes flared beneath her touch, responding to the faint echo of the sigil still etched into her skin. The ground trembled, a low, keening hum vibrating through her bones.

Adrian's voice was soft behind her. "You don't have to do this alone."

She turned, meeting his gaze. "Yes, I do."

His eyes darkened, not with anger, but fear—the kind that comes when you realize there's nothing you can do to stop what's coming.

Selene reached for him, her fingers brushing his cheek, memorizing the warmth of his skin, the rough stubble beneath her touch. "Thank you," she whispered, though the words felt too small for everything he'd been.

Adrian's hand covered hers, his grip fierce. "Don't thank me. Just come back."

She didn't promise. She couldn't.

Instead, she turned back to the gate, drawing a ragged breath as the runes ignited in a blinding surge of light. The stone groaned, splitting open like a wound, revealing not darkness—but **endless, blinding white.**

The **Veil.**

She stepped through without looking back, the tether between worlds snapping taut.

And for the first time, she felt *weightless*—unbound, suspended between life and death.

But even here, Selene Ward carried one truth with her:

She was not here to survive.

She was here to end it.

--------

The air near the **Veil Gate** pulsed with an unnatural tension, as if the very fabric of reality strained to hold itself together. The ancient stone arch, carved with runes older than memory, glimmered faintly, responding to Selene's presence like a heartbeat syncing with her own fragile rhythm. The faint glow of her **sigil** had diminished, leaving behind a dull ache—a reminder that her time was slipping through her fingers like water.

In the dim glow of flickering lanterns, **Elias** laid out crude diagrams on a cracked slab of stone, his fingers tracing the symbols with clinical precision. His face was cast in shadows, but his voice remained steady, a thin thread of authority in the oppressive silence.

"Once you cross into the Veil," he began, glancing at Selene, "you won't just face the Council's power or the Veilborn's influence. The Veil doesn't play by the rules of this world. It strips you down to the marrow. Your fears, your regrets—everything you've buried—it'll drag it to the surface."

Selene stared at the sketches, but her mind was miles away, tangled in thoughts she couldn't afford to unpack. "I'm not afraid of shadows."

Elias gave a hollow chuckle. "It's not the shadows you should fear. It's the light they leave behind."

She didn't respond. What was there to say? Fear was a luxury she'd burned out of herself long ago.

Adrian stood a few feet away, his gaze distant, arms crossed as if he could physically hold himself together. The silence between them had grown louder since the escape, thick with words unsaid. Selene felt it pressing in, a weight she refused to acknowledge.

But tonight, it seemed Adrian wasn't going to let her ignore it.

As Elias moved to gather supplies, Adrian crossed the space between them, his steps slow but determined. His face was drawn, shadows etched beneath his eyes—not just from exhaustion, but from something deeper, something raw.

"Selene," he started, his voice softer than usual, lacking its usual edge of deflection.

She didn't look at him. Instead, she double-checked the blade strapped to her thigh, fingers trembling slightly—not from fear of the battle ahead, but from what she knew was coming in his voice.

"Don't," she muttered, tightening the strap with unnecessary force.

Adrian didn't stop. He stepped closer, his hand brushing against hers briefly, a touch too fleeting to be casual. "I have to say this."

She swallowed hard, her chest tight. "No, you don't."

His hand caught her wrist gently, his fingers warm despite the chill in the cavernous space. She finally met his gaze, and it hit her like a punch to the ribs—*the truth* reflected in his eyes, raw and unguarded.

"I can't lose you," he whispered, his voice breaking slightly, like it had been holding back years of weight.

Selene's breath hitched, a fissure cracking through the walls she'd built around herself. She yanked her hand free, stepping back as if distance could dull the sharpness of his words.

"Stop," she snapped, her voice harder than she meant it to be. "This isn't the time."

Adrian's jaw tightened, but he didn't step forward again. "There won't be a 'later,' Selene. You know that."

She turned away, pretending to check her gear, anything to avoid the look in his eyes. "Then don't make it harder than it already is."

Silence settled between them, thicker than before.

Adrian finally spoke, his voice quieter now. "You think shutting me out makes it easier to lose me?"

She didn't answer. She couldn't.

Because the truth was, it did.

Elias's voice cut through the tension. "It's time."

Selene forced her feet to move, her heart pounding not from fear of what awaited in the Veil—but from what she'd left unsaid.

She walked toward the gate without looking back, her chest hollow and burning at the same time.

The Veil wasn't the only thing she was afraid to face.

--------

The **Veil Gate** roared to life with a sound that was both deafening and eerily silent, like the universe inhaling and forgetting how to exhale. Blinding light spilled from the arch, tendrils of energy reaching out like fingers desperate to pull Selene through. She stood at the threshold, her body aching, her heart pounding—not from fear of what lay beyond, but from everything she'd left unsaid.

She took one step forward, then another.

And the world unraveled.

---

When Selene opened her eyes, she wasn't sure if she'd blinked—or if reality itself had fractured.

The city around her resembled **Nightrift**, but it was wrong. The buildings were twisted, leaning at impossible angles, their shadows stretching far too long, even though there was no sun. The sky above was a swirling canvas of bruised purples and sickly greens, veins of light pulsing like cracks in glass. Streets bled into each other, looping in ways that defied logic, as if time had melted and pooled in the corners.

Selene stood alone in the middle of it all, the faint glow of her sigil flickering against the pale skin beneath her collar. She drew a shaky breath, the air thick with something sharp and metallic—*not blood,* but close.

"Adrian?" she called out, her voice swallowed by the heavy silence.

No answer.

She took a tentative step forward, her boots echoing louder than they should. The ground beneath her was solid but felt unstable, like walking on the surface of a frozen lake that could crack at any second.

Then, she heard it.

A whisper.

*"Selene…"*

She spun around, but no one was there. Just the endless, twisted city, and her own ragged breath.

The whispers grew louder, layered, like voices stacked on top of each other—familiar voices.

*Mendez.*
*Captain* *Holt.*
*Adrian.*

She clenched her fists, shaking her head. "No. You're not real."

But the whispers didn't stop.

*"You* *left* *us."*
*"You* *failed."*
*"You're nothing without us."*

Selene's chest tightened. She pressed her hands over her ears, but the voices were inside her head now, burrowing deep.

Then, a new voice—smooth, cold, and unmistakably **not** human.

*"We are not your ghosts, Selene Ward."*

She froze.

The shadows in front of her twisted, peeling away from the cracked pavement like smoke given shape. They coalesced into a figure—tall, androgynous, its form shifting like liquid darkness, eyes glowing faintly with an unnatural light.

A **Veilborn**.

Selene instinctively reached for her weapon, but her holster was empty. *Of course,* she thought bitterly. *Nothing works here.*

The Veilborn tilted its head, as if amused. *"You don't need a weapon here. What can you kill when everything is already dead?"*

Selene squared her shoulders, forcing her voice to steady. "What do you want?"

It stepped closer, its form flickering like static. *"Not want. Offer."*

She glared. "I'm not here to make deals."

*"No deals,"* it replied, circling her like a predator with no need to rush. *"Only truths. You've come seeking answers, haven't you? About the contracts. The Council. Yourself."*

Selene's jaw clenched. She hated that it was right.

*"We can give you what you seek,"* the Veilborn whispered, stopping inches from her face. Its eyes weren't eyes—not really—just voids filled with flickering echoes of light. *"All you have to do is listen."*

She swallowed hard, her heart pounding in her ears. "And why would you help me?"

*"Because you're already ours,"* it replied softly.

Selene's breath hitched.

The words slid under her skin like glass shards.

She wanted to deny it, to scream that she belonged to no one—but the faint pulse of her fading sigil told a different story.

The Veilborn extended a hand, its fingers shifting like ink in water. *"Let us show you."*

Selene hesitated, her hand hovering just inches from the darkness.

She wasn't afraid of what it would show her.

She was afraid it would be the truth.

# Chapter 12
# The Heart of the Veil

The **Veil** shifted around Selene like a living thing, constantly morphing—its landscapes folding in on themselves, spiraling into impossible geometries, only to flatten again into eerie, familiar streets. She stumbled forward, her breath ragged, disoriented by the crushing sense of déjà vu wrapped around something grotesquely *wrong*.

She wasn't just walking through a place.

She was walking through **herself.**

The first vision hit without warning.

One blink—and suddenly she was standing in the warm glow of a small apartment bathed in morning light. The smell of coffee lingered in the air, mingling with the faint, familiar scent of rain-soaked streets outside. A soft voice called from the other room.

**"Selene? You're going to be late."**

She turned her head slowly, her heart seizing in her chest.

**Adrian** stepped into view—not the scarred, broken man she'd left behind in the rebellion, but *Adrian as he was before.* Hair tousled from sleep, eyes soft and unguarded, wearing nothing but a faded T-shirt and a smile meant just for her.

Selene's fingers twitched at her side. *No. This isn't real.*

But it *felt* real.

She looked down. No weapon. No sigil. Just bare skin, unmarked and whole. A life untouched by the Council, by death, by pain.

Adrian crossed the room, brushing a kiss to her temple. "You always get that look when you overthink."

She swallowed hard. "What... is this?"

He chuckled softly, pulling her close. "This is *us*. You didn't leave. You didn't chase ghosts. You stayed."

His arms around her felt like home. A part of her—the part that still ached with every loss—wanted to collapse into it. To *believe*.

But then she saw it—a flicker in the corner of her vision. The light dimmed, shadows creeping where they shouldn't. **The Veilborn's influence.** A crack in the illusion.

Selene jerked back, her breath sharp. "You're not him."

Adrian's face twisted—not with anger, but disappointment. "Why fight it, Selene? You could be *happy*. Isn't that what you wanted?"

She clenched her fists, grounding herself in the pain she'd earned. "No. I wanted the truth."

The illusion shattered like glass.

She dropped to her knees, gasping as the real world—or whatever passed for it here—reasserted itself. The Veil writhed around her, landscapes flickering like broken film reels.

But it wasn't done with her.

The second vision came just as fast.

Now she stood in a crisp, sterile office. The Council's emblem gleamed on the walls. She was dressed in black—an enforcer's uniform. Her reflection in the glass showed eyes void of warmth, the faint glow of a *perfect* sigil etched over her heart, unblemished and whole.

A voice echoed from behind her. **Captain Holt.** Alive, standing tall.

"Well done, Agent Ward," he said with a smile that never reached his eyes. "You've been our finest weapon."

Selene's breath hitched. The weight of control pressed against her chest like a vice.

*No.*

She spun, drawing a weapon that had appeared in her hand without thought, and shot him point-blank. The illusion shattered before the bullet hit.

She collapsed again, her heart pounding. Her mind felt frayed, pulled at from every angle.

**"You're unraveling,"** the Veilborn whispered, its voice curling around her like smoke. *"What's the point of fighting when you could have peace?"*

Selene forced herself to her feet, her knees trembling. "Peace isn't real if you have to bleed out your soul to get it."

The Veil shifted once more—this time, no illusion. Just Selene standing alone in an endless void.

No walls. No memories.

Just *herself*.

She clenched her fists, her voice raw. "Is that it? Cheap tricks? Illusions?"

The Veilborn's laughter slithered through the dark. **"No, Selene Ward. That was the gift. The real fight starts now."**

She braced herself.

Because she wasn't done fighting.

--------

The void shifted.

After the barrage of illusions, the Veil settled into an eerie stillness, the oppressive darkness giving way to a faint, pulsing glow on the horizon. Selene trudged toward it, each step heavier than the last, as if the very fabric of this place resisted her presence. Her body ached—not from wounds, but from something deeper, a slow erosion of her will, her essence.

She stumbled into a clearing carved from the emptiness itself. The ground was slick like glass, reflecting fractured versions of herself—one with bloodstained hands, another with hollow eyes, and yet another wearing the crisp uniform of a Council enforcer. She didn't look at them long.

Instead, her gaze fixed on the figure standing at the center.

A woman.

She wasn't like the other illusions—too vivid, too solid, with shadows that obeyed natural laws. Her presence radiated something different. **Aurelia.** Tall, ethereal, her features sharp and luminous, with hair cascading like liquid silver. But her eyes... Selene knew those eyes. Not the color, not the shape—but the emptiness behind them. The look of someone who'd been hollowed out.

Selene's hand instinctively went to her hip, but of course, there was no weapon. Just her defiance.

"Who are you?" Selene rasped, her voice raw from screaming into empty spaces.

The woman turned slowly, her gaze piercing but devoid of malice. "I am what's left."

Cryptic. Typical.

Selene squared her shoulders. "That's not an answer."

Aurelia stepped forward, her bare feet making no sound on the glass-like surface. "I was the first. The prototype. The original contract."

Selene's pulse quickened. "You're bound?"

A faint smile curved Aurelia's lips—one filled with bitter nostalgia rather than warmth. "Was. But not in the way you understand. Before the Council. Before your world even knew how to name its gods or its fears."

Selene's jaw tightened. "What does that mean?"

Aurelia gestured around them. "The contracts were never meant for humans. They were designed by the **Veilborn**—tools to harvest, to control. Not bodies. Not souls. *Emotions.* That's what they feed on. Fear. Love. Grief. Passion. The raw essence of what makes you human."

Selene's breath caught, her mind racing. *Harvest.*

"All this time…" she whispered. "We thought the contracts were about power, binding people to each other."

Aurelia's expression darkened. "No. They're about *binding people to the Veil*. The Council figured that out early, but instead of resisting, they offered themselves willingly. They became the Veilborn's stewards, trading your freedom for influence. For immortality."

Selene felt like the floor had dropped beneath her.

"The Council is just…" She struggled to find the words.

"Puppets," Aurelia finished softly. "Strings woven from ambition and fear."

Selene clenched her fists. "And the sigils?"

"Anchors," Aurelia replied. "Each one a tether to the Veil. The stronger the emotion tied to it, the stronger the pull. Marriage, loyalty, vengeance—all perfect conduits."

Selene's mind flashed with images—**the dead couples**, the **fading sigils**, **Adrian's face** after every argument, every loss. The weight of it hit her all at once.

"So that's why I'm unraveling," she muttered, her fingers brushing against the faint pulse beneath her collarbone. "I'm not just connected. I'm a battery."

Aurelia nodded. "And when you're drained, you'll be discarded. Like the others."

Selene's breath grew ragged, not from fear, but rage.

"And what about you?" she snapped. "Why are you telling me this?"

Aurelia's gaze softened for the first time. "Because I was like you once. I thought I could fight it. Thought I could change it."

Selene stepped closer, her voice low and fierce. "And?"

Aurelia's smile faded. "I lost."

Selene stared at her, the words sinking in. The truth was a weight, but it didn't crush her.

It fueled her.

"Good," she whispered, straightening her spine. "Because I don't plan on losing."

Aurelia's eyes glimmered, something like hope—or maybe regret—reflected in them. "Then don't make the same mistake I did."

Selene's heart pounded, her pulse syncing with the faint thrum beneath her feet.

She wasn't just fighting for herself anymore.

She was fighting for everyone who'd ever signed their life away, not knowing what price they'd truly pay.

The Veil shifted again, reshaping itself into something eerily familiar—a distorted echo of Selene's old apartment. The peeling wallpaper, the flickering overhead light, even the faint scent of stale coffee and rain-soaked pavement. It wasn't real. She knew that. But it *felt* real, and that was the point.

She stepped inside cautiously, her footsteps muffled against the warped wooden floor. The room was suffused with a dim, amber glow, casting long shadows that seemed to stretch and curl unnaturally, like fingers reaching for her.

At the center of the room, facing the cracked mirror above the fireplace, stood a figure.

Selene froze.

The woman turned slowly, and Selene's breath caught.

It was **her**—but not. The doppelgänger's eyes were colder, darker, hollowed out like something had been carved away. The faint outline of a perfect, unblemished sigil pulsed faintly beneath her collarbone, stark against pale skin.

The reflection tilted its head, studying Selene with a faint smirk. "Took you long enough."

Selene's jaw clenched. "You're not me."

"Oh, but I am," the doppelgänger replied smoothly, stepping closer. Her movements were fluid, too precise—like she was a marionette pretending to be human. "I'm everything you've buried. Every doubt, every failure, every fear you refused to face."

Selene squared her shoulders, her fists tightening. "I've faced worse than you."

The reflection chuckled, a hollow, grating sound. "No, you haven't. You've run from me your entire life. Chased distractions. Buried yourself in duty. In guilt. Even in him." She took another step, closing the space between them. "Adrian, Mendez, the rebellion—it's all just noise to drown me out."

Selene's heart hammered, but she kept her face stone-cold. "You think saying it makes it true?"

The doppelgänger's grin widened, predatory and sharp. "I don't have to make it true. *You* already did. Every time you pushed people away. Every time you chose the fight over the people who cared about you."

Selene felt the sting of the words, but she refused to flinch. She'd lived with those thoughts for years, letting them fester in the dark corners of her mind. But standing here, facing them, she realized something.

They weren't truths.

They were *fears*.

And fear was just a story you told yourself when you forgot who you were.

Selene took a step forward, her voice low but steady. "You're not here to help me. You're here to keep me small. To make me forget who I am."

The doppelgänger's smile faltered, just slightly.

Selene pressed on. "I'm not afraid of you."

"*You should be,*" the reflection snapped, its face twisting with sudden rage. "Without me, you're nothing. You're broken. Weak. Just another lost soul pretending to be strong."

Selene shook her head. "No. I'm strong *because* of you."

The doppelgänger blinked, confusion flickering across her face.

"I'm strong because I've been broken. Because I've been afraid. Because I've lost and still kept going." Selene's voice grew stronger with each word, her heart pounding with defiant clarity. "You're not my shadow. You're my proof."

The reflection snarled and lunged.

But Selene didn't flinch.

Instead, she stepped into the attack, grabbing the doppelgänger's wrist and pulling her close, their faces inches apart. "You don't win by being louder," she whispered. "You win by surviving."

The room shattered around them like glass, the illusion crumbling into fragments of light.

Selene stood alone again, breathless but unbowed.

She pressed her hand to her chest, feeling the faint pulse of her fading sigil—but now it wasn't just a mark.

It was a reminder.

Her strength didn't come from denying her fears.

It came from *embracing* them.

And she was far from done.

# Chapter 13
## A Bargain Written in Blood

The Veil was a labyrinth of fractured realities, where time folded in on itself and shadows whispered secrets meant to be forgotten. **Adrian** had no map, no guide—only sheer determination and the echo of Selene's name reverberating in his mind like a drumbeat. The air was thick, not with oxygen but with memories—his own and those of strangers long gone, blurring into indistinguishable fragments.

His breath came in ragged gasps as he pushed forward, the stolen sigil Elias had crafted burning against his skin, barely enough to keep him tethered. The boundary between his thoughts and the Veil's influence thinned with each step, and he felt pieces of himself peeling away like brittle parchment. But none of it mattered.

*Selene was here.*

And she was facing something he couldn't leave her to fight alone.

The world around him shifted—streets melting into endless corridors, ceilings collapsing into starless skies. Until, suddenly, he saw her.

**Selene.**

She stood at the center of a vast, open expanse where the ground cracked like glass beneath her boots. The sky was a churning mass of darkness, streaked with veins of crimson light, pulsating like the exposed flesh of something alive. And before her loomed a creature that defied logic—a towering entity composed of shifting shadows, its form fluid, morphing between shapes, its voice a chorus of whispers layered into one unbearable sound.

The **Veilborn Sovereign.**

Adrian didn't think. He ran.

"Selene!" His voice was raw, shredded by the weight of this place, but it reached her.

She turned, her face a mask of exhaustion and defiance. Her eyes met his—and for a second, just a second, the darkness seemed to falter.

"Adrian?" she breathed, disbelief threading through the ragged edge of her voice.

The Sovereign's form shifted, its many eyes—if they could be called that—snapping toward him. The air grew heavier, pressing against his chest, threatening to crush the very breath from his lungs.

Selene's expression hardened. "You idiot. You weren't supposed to follow me."

He stumbled to her side, gasping. "You really thought… I'd let you face this alone?"

She shook her head, but there was no time for arguments. The Sovereign's voice seeped into their minds, bypassing language altogether.

*"Two broken souls, clinging to each other like driftwood in a drowning sea."*

Adrian gritted his teeth, steadying himself. "Yeah? Well, maybe that's all we need."

Selene's hand brushed against his briefly, a fleeting connection sparking in the darkness. She faced the Sovereign, her voice strong despite the tremor in her chest. "I know what you are."

The Sovereign shifted, shadows coiling tighter. *"Then you know what I can offer."*

Adrian's fingers curled into fists. "We're not here to bargain."

The creature's laughter was a soundless quake, rattling the very ground beneath their feet. *"You misunderstand, fragile thing. A bargain has already been made. Written in blood, etched in soul. You are merely fulfilling its terms."*

Selene took a step forward, her shoulders squared. "I'm not here to fulfill anything. I'm here to end it."

The Sovereign's shadows writhed, stretching toward her like tendrils, but Adrian stepped between them without thinking, drawing the faint flicker of a ward from his jacket—a desperate charm, weak but fueled by sheer will.

"Not today," he hissed.

Selene pulled him back gently but firmly. "I've got this."

Adrian's heart hammered, but he nodded. "I know."

She stepped forward again, her voice cutting through the darkness like a blade. "You feed on fear, on pain, on control. But here's the thing—those aren't weaknesses. They're fuel. And I've got more than enough to burn you down."

The Sovereign lunged, its form exploding into a hurricane of shadow and sound.

Adrian grabbed her hand, anchoring her as the world collapsed around them.

Whatever came next, they would face it together.

--------

The Veil twisted around them, the fabric of reality fraying with every breath Selene took. The **Sovereign** loomed like a void stitched together by shadows and whispers, its form constantly shifting—faces flickering in and out of existence, some familiar, some horrifyingly foreign. The very air around it pulsed with a dark rhythm, like the heartbeat of something ancient and wrong.

Selene stood shoulder-to-shoulder with **Adrian**, her fingers still wrapped tightly around his hand, grounding herself in the reality of his presence. But even that anchor felt fragile here.

The Sovereign's voice seeped into her mind—not spoken aloud, but planted directly into her thoughts, heavy and undeniable.

*"A choice must be made."*

Selene's jaw tightened. "I'm not interested in your games."

*"It's not a game."* The Sovereign's form shifted again, sprouting tendrils that reached lazily toward the empty sky. *"It's balance. The scales are tipped, the threads frayed. Humanity's debt must be paid."*

Selene could feel it—the truth woven into its words, even if every instinct screamed to reject it. The contracts, the sigils, the endless drain of lives—*they* were the price. And now the Veil wanted its final payment.

The Sovereign turned its void-like gaze toward Adrian, its tendrils curling like smoke. *"One soul. That's all it takes. His."*

Selene's breath hitched.

Adrian stepped slightly in front of her, his voice low but steady. "Of course."

She whipped her head toward him. "*What?*"

He met her gaze, his eyes softer than she'd ever seen them. "It makes sense. I'm already half gone after everything with the Council. You know it."

Selene shook her head, her heart racing. "No. Don't you *dare*."

Adrian gave a bitter laugh, his hand tightening around hers. "Selene, look around you. This is bigger than us."

"*I don't care!*" she snapped, her voice breaking under the weight of everything she'd held back. "You don't get to decide that. Not for me."

The Sovereign's voice slithered between them, colder than ice. "*Sacrifice him, and the contracts will crumble. The drain will end. Humanity will be free.*"

Selene's chest felt like it was collapsing. The logical part of her—the detective, the fighter—understood the math. *One life for millions.*

But this wasn't a case. This wasn't a statistic.

This was *Adrian*.

His hand cupped her face gently, thumb brushing over the curve of her cheek. "Selene," he whispered, "you can do this. You're stronger than me. Stronger than all of this."

Tears burned in her eyes, but she refused to let them fall. "Don't you dare tell me I'm strong like it's supposed to make this okay."

His smile was soft, tinged with sadness. "I'm not trying to make it okay. I'm just trying to make it *matter*."

She shook her head, stepping back, her hands trembling. "No. No, there's another way. There *has* to be."

The Sovereign's shadows coiled tighter, sensing her weakness. *"There is not. Choose. Or lose both."*

Selene's knees buckled, but she caught herself.

And then she remembered.

*The Veil thrives on fear, on pain, on control.*

This wasn't a choice.

It was a trap.

Her eyes snapped open, fury burning away the despair. She faced the Sovereign, her voice razor-sharp. "You're not offering a bargain. You're just trying to break me."

The Sovereign stilled, as if surprised.

Selene stepped forward, her heart pounding with defiant clarity. "I don't accept your terms."

The Sovereign's form convulsed, rage rippling through its shadowed body. *"Refusal is death."*

Selene's lips curled into a fierce smile. "Then I'll die fighting."

She turned, grabbed Adrian's hand, and held tight—not as an anchor, but as a weapon.

They faced the darkness together.

Not broken.

*Whole.*

--------

The Veil pulsed like a living wound, its tendrils of shadow coiling tighter, feeding off Selene's hesitation. The Sovereign loomed, its voice an unholy chorus vibrating through the marrow of her bones.

"Choose."

Selene stood between the monstrous entity and Adrian, her heart pounding like war drums in her chest. The ultimatum echoed in her mind—Adrian's soul or the world's slow death.

But she saw it now for what it really was: a trap woven from fear, designed to strip away her agency until all that was left was surrender.

She exhaled slowly, grounding herself.

"No," she said softly.

The Sovereign's form convulsed, shadows stretching and recoiling like a beast provoked. "You cannot refuse. Balance must be restored."

Selene took a step forward, her voice growing stronger. "You think power comes from forcing people to make impossible choices. But that's not power. That's desperation."

Adrian's grip on her wrist tightened. "Selene, don't—"

She turned to him, cutting him off with a look that said everything words couldn't. "I'm not sacrificing you. I'm not choosing between you and the rest of the world."

His voice cracked, rough with emotion. "Then what are you doing?"

She squeezed his hand, her thumb brushing over his knuckles—one last anchor to everything real. "I'm making *my* choice."

Adrian's eyes widened. "Selene—"

But she was already stepping forward, away from him, toward the abyss.

The Sovereign's tendrils reached out greedily, sensing her resolve.

Selene stood tall, her voice clear and fierce. "You want a soul? Take *mine*."

Adrian's shout echoed behind her. "*No!*"

She didn't turn back.

"This isn't a sacrifice," she continued, her gaze locked on the churning void of the Sovereign's form. "This is a rebellion."

The Veil trembled, its fabric warping under the weight of her defiance.

"You cannot offer what must be taken," the Sovereign hissed.

"That's where you're wrong," Selene snarled. "*I'm not offering it. I'm giving it. Freely.*"

And that was the flaw—the crack in the Sovereign's perfect system.

The contracts thrived on coercion, manipulation, control. But **free will**? That was chaos. Unpredictable. Untamable.

Selene pressed her hand to her chest, where the faint outline of her fading sigil pulsed one last time. She ripped it free—not with magic, not with force, but with sheer determination. The mark disintegrated into ash, scattering into the Veil's currents like defiant sparks.

The Sovereign shrieked, its form fracturing, unable to comprehend the act. "This is not balance!"

Selene smiled through the pain ripping her apart from the inside out. "No. It's freedom."

Adrian's voice was the last thing she heard before the light swallowed everything.

"*Selene!*"

When the dust settled, the Veil was silent.

No contracts. No Sovereign.

Just echoes.

And the undeniable proof that true power was never about control.

It was about the choice to defy it.

# Chapter 14
# The Breaking Point

Selene drifted, untethered from everything that had once anchored her. There was no pain now, only a vast emptiness, like floating in deep water with no surface in sight. Her senses dulled, consciousness slipping like grains of sand through open fingers.

Then—light.

It wasn't harsh or blinding but warm, golden, and soft, wrapping around her like a distant memory. Slowly, images bled into focus, hazy at first, then sharpening with startling clarity.

She stood on the edge of a city. Not the twisted reflection of Nightrift she'd known, not the fractured landscapes of the Veil. This was real—or at least *felt* real. The sky stretched wide, painted in hues of dawn, casting long shadows over streets filled with people. She recognized none of them, yet every face told a story she somehow knew.

There were no sigils glowing faintly beneath collars. No Council enforcers lurking in the corners, their eyes sharp with suspicion. The weight that had pressed against the city's spine for generations was gone.

Adrian's voice drifted to her, faint but unmistakable. "You did it."

She turned, expecting to see him standing beside her, but there was only air and that persistent warmth against her skin. She wasn't really *there*. She was watching—an observer to the world she'd left behind.

In the distance, the **Council's stronghold** lay in ruins. Its once-imposing towers now crumbled, vines reclaiming stone and steel. The air buzzed with the sound of voices—not chants of rebellion, but laughter, conversation, life unfurling freely, unchained from invisible bonds.

Selene moved through the streets, unseen, unheard, her steps weightless. She passed a child playing with a makeshift kite, the string tangled around tiny fingers, no sigil etched into soft skin. A woman, sleeves rolled up, painted over faded Council propaganda with vibrant colors—swirls of blue and orange that seemed to hum with defiance.

And then she heard them—fragments of voices woven into the city's pulse.

"They're gone," a man murmured, awe thick in his tone. "The contracts… they just disappeared."

"I thought I'd feel empty without it," another voice replied, softer, trembling with emotion. "But I feel… like me."

Selene's chest tightened, though she wasn't sure if it was sorrow, pride, or something between the two.

Adrian's voice again, closer this time. "You always carried the weight for everyone else."

She swallowed hard, her gaze lifting to the horizon where the first light of dawn crept over the ruins.

"What's left of me now?" she whispered into the void.

His answer was soft, but steady. "Hope."

Selene's vision blurred, not from tears—she couldn't cry here—but from something deeper unraveling inside her. She saw flashes—Mendez standing tall among a crowd, Elias scribbling frantic notes with a grin that hadn't touched his face in years, rebels who no longer had to rebel because there was nothing left to fight against.

Freedom. Not given. *Earned.*

But as she turned back, hoping—*needing*—to see Adrian's face, there was only the fading light and the echo of his voice.

"You're not gone. You're part of this."

The warmth began to fade, replaced by a distant pull, like the tide receding from the shore.

Selene's breath hitched.

Was this it?

Her consciousness drifted on the edge, balanced between nothingness and something she couldn't define. But the last thing she felt wasn't fear.

It was peace.

--------

The Veil was quieter now, but not empty. It pulsed with the echoes of what had been—a world unmaking itself in the absence of the Sovereign's control. Shadows no longer whispered with the same venom, their voices faded to distant murmurs, like waves receding from the shore after a storm.

But **Adrian** didn't hear them. He didn't care.

All he could think about was **Selene.**

He stood in the hollow where she had fallen, the ground scarred, fractured like glass beneath his feet. The place where her light had burned the brightest—and disappeared. The memory of her final words, her defiant stand, played on repeat in his mind.

*"I'm not offering it. I'm giving it. Freely."*

His chest felt hollow, carved out by the absence of her voice, her presence, the stubborn fire she carried even when the world tried to snuff it out. But Adrian refused to believe this was the end. She couldn't just be *gone*.

Not her.

Not Selene.

His fists clenched, nails digging into his palms until they bled, the sting grounding him. "You're still here," he whispered into the emptiness, his voice ragged. "You have to be."

But there was no answer.

The Veil didn't respond to desperation—not in the way he wanted.

Adrian fell to his knees, the grief threatening to drown him. His head dropped, breaths coming in harsh gasps, as if the very act of breathing without her was too heavy.

Then, through the suffocating silence, he heard it.

A whisper.

Not from the Veil. Not from the shadows.

But from somewhere deeper.

*Selene.*

It wasn't her voice exactly—more like the *memory* of it, buried beneath layers of pain and stubborn hope.

Adrian's eyes snapped open.

This wasn't just grief. It was a tether.

A connection.

His connection to her.

"She's not gone," he muttered, rising to his feet with shaky resolve. "She's not."

The Veil shifted around him, reacting to his will. It wasn't like before when it had fought to dominate him. Now it felt different—like it *recognized* him, or maybe recognized what he carried: love that refused to let go.

Adrian stumbled forward, following the faintest pull, like chasing the thread of a forgotten song. The landscape twisted, reality folding in on itself—fragments of places, memories, echoes. His vision blurred with images that weren't his: Selene's childhood home, the cracked precinct walls, the fractured reflection in her bathroom mirror.

But he pressed on.

"Selene!" he shouted, his voice raw, breaking against the Veil's shifting walls. "You're not done. You hear me? *I'm not done!*"

The air trembled.

A flicker of light, faint and distant, pulsed like a dying star on the horizon.

Adrian's heart surged. He ran toward it, stumbling, falling, but never stopping. The closer he got, the stronger the pull grew—not the cold grip of the Veil's magic, but something warmer, something fierce.

Love.

When he reached the light, he collapsed beside it, digging into the emptiness with trembling hands until he found her—Selene's form curled in on itself, her face pale, eyes closed, as if sleep had claimed her instead of death.

"No," he whispered, cradling her in his arms, his tears falling freely now. "No, no, no…"

Her body was cold, but he refused to believe she was gone.

"Selene," he choked out, pressing his forehead to hers. "You fought for everyone else. Let me fight for *you* now."

He didn't know if she could hear him.

Didn't care.

"I'm not leaving you here," he whispered, his voice fierce even through the trembling. "You're the one who told me choices matter. *This* is mine. I choose you."

The Veil trembled again, reacting not to magic, not to spells, but to the sheer force of his will—his refusal to let her go.

The light beneath her skin flickered.

Adrian's breath hitched. "That's it. Come back to me. Please."

Her fingers twitched.

And for the first time since she'd fallen, Selene's eyes opened—dim, unfocused, but alive.

Adrian laughed, a sound choked with relief and disbelief. "Hey. There you are."

Selene's voice was a rasp, barely audible. "Took you long enough."

Adrian pulled her closer, resting his forehead against hers, tears mixing with laughter. "You're never going to hear the end of this."

And she didn't argue.

Because she was finally home.

--------

The Veil writhed around them, less like a place now and more like a living thing—its shadows thinning, unraveling in threads of darkness, as if reality itself was struggling to hold form. **Adrian** cradled Selene's fragile body, her skin cold beneath his trembling fingers, but he refused to believe this was all that was left of her.

She was here. Somewhere beneath the exhaustion, beneath the quiet, beneath the fragile flicker of life that felt like it could be snuffed out with a breath.

Adrian's heart pounded in his chest, raw with a desperation he didn't bother to hide. His hands cupped her face, thumbs brushing over the faint traces of the sigil that once burned bright and fierce beneath her skin. Now, it was nothing more than a shadow—a scar left behind by all the battles she'd fought.

"Selene," he whispered, his voice cracking under the weight of her name.

Nothing.

No flicker of consciousness. No sharp retort, no stubborn glare. Just silence.

But Adrian wasn't here to mourn. He was here to fight.

Not for her.

*With* her.

He closed his eyes, drawing a shaky breath, willing his mind to reach past the physical—to find her where words couldn't. The Veil responded, pulling him deeper into its fractured heart, dragging him down until there was nothing left but darkness and the echo of his own heartbeat.

Then—faint, distant—*her.*

A flicker of light. Fragile. Fractured.

He followed it, pushing through the suffocating void until he found her: Selene, not as the woman who had faced down gods and Council enforcers, but as a shard of herself—fragmented, lost, suspended in the emptiness like a star struggling to burn.

Adrian reached for her, his heart in his throat. "Selene."

Her head lifted slightly, her eyes distant, unfocused. She didn't recognize him. She wasn't *there*.

Not fully.

"Hey," he said softly, kneeling beside her, his fingers ghosting over her hand. "You don't get to disappear on me. Not now. Not after everything."

No response.

Adrian swallowed hard, the lump in his throat threatening to choke him. He leaned closer, his forehead resting against hers, his voice dropping to a fragile whisper.

"I thought if I found you, I could save you," he admitted, the words spilling out like confession. "But that was never the truth, was it?"

His breath hitched, tears blurring his vision.

"You don't need me to save you," he whispered. "You never did."

His hands gripped hers, grounding himself even as the Veil pulsed, trying to pull her further away.

"I was just too scared to believe you could save yourself," he breathed, his voice breaking. "Because if you could... it meant I had to let you."

The darkness trembled.

Selene's fingers twitched.

Adrian's heart stuttered.

"That's the thing about love," he murmured, a shaky smile tugging at the corner of his mouth. "It's not about holding on. It's about knowing when to let go."

He closed his eyes, pressing one last kiss to her forehead, his voice steady despite the tears. "So I'm letting you go. But I'm not giving up. I believe in you, Selene. I always have."

The words settled in the silence, fragile as glass.

Then—light.

A pulse from within her, faint at first, then growing stronger, brighter, burning through the darkness like a spark finding kindling.

Selene gasped, her eyes snapping open, clarity flooding back with the force of a crashing wave.

Adrian's breath hitched, his chest tight with disbelief and relief. "Hey," he whispered, a tear slipping down his cheek. "There you are."

Selene's fingers tightened around his.

Her voice was hoarse, barely audible, but filled with quiet defiance. "Took you long enough."

Adrian laughed, breathless, his forehead resting against hers. "Yeah, well. You're hard to keep up with."

The Veil around them began to shatter, the final bond breaking—not with force, not with magic, but with the simple, unstoppable power of belief.

They were whole again.

Together.

# Chapter 15
# Echoes After the Fall

Selene woke to the faint glow of morning light seeping through the blinds, casting thin, golden stripes across the cracked ceiling. She blinked, disoriented, her body stiff as if she'd been asleep for years instead of... *how long?*

She sat up slowly, her breath shallow, eyes scanning the room.

Her apartment.

Or something that *looked* like it.

The familiar chipped paint on the walls, the coffee mug still resting on the windowsill, half-empty. But there was something wrong—or maybe something *too right*. The air felt lighter, the usual tension she'd grown so accustomed to was gone, like a pressure she never realized she'd been holding had finally released.

Her hand drifted to her chest.

The sigil was gone.

In its place, a faint scar—a thin, jagged line etched over her heart, pale against her skin. She traced it with trembling fingers, not out of grief, but recognition. A mark not of ownership, but of survival.

She stood, her legs shaky beneath her, and crossed the room. The city stretched beyond her window, bathed in the soft light of dawn. But Nightrift wasn't the same. Gone were the towering surveillance drones that once hovered like vultures. No more oppressive banners bearing the Council's emblem. Just… life. Unremarkable. Ordinary.

Free.

Her breath fogged the glass slightly as she leaned in closer, watching people below—laughing, talking, *existing* without fear. It felt surreal.

A voice broke the silence.

"Thought you'd sleep forever."

Selene spun around, her heart leaping.

Adrian stood in the doorway, leaning casually against the frame like he'd always belonged there, like he hadn't crossed dimensions to pull her back from the edge. His eyes were softer now, shadows still lingering in their depths, but tempered by something warmer.

She tried to speak, but her throat tightened.

Adrian stepped into the room, his hands tucked into his jacket pockets. "You've been out for a couple of days. Elias thought you might punch me when you woke up."

Selene managed a dry smile. "Lucky for you, I'm too tired."

Adrian smirked, but it didn't reach his eyes. There was something unsaid between them, heavy but not oppressive—like the quiet after a storm.

Selene's gaze drifted back to the window. "It's different."

Adrian followed her eyes. "Yeah. The Council's gone. The contracts dissolved the moment…" He trailed off, his voice catching slightly. "The moment you broke the bond."

She didn't respond right away. The silence stretched, filled only by the faint hum of the city below.

Finally, she asked softly, "And us?"

Adrian's jaw tensed. He crossed the room, stopping just short of her, their reflections faintly overlapping in the glass.

"I don't know," he admitted. "But we're here."

Selene nodded slowly, her fingers brushing over the scar again.

A reminder.

Of everything lost. And everything saved.

She turned to face him fully, her voice low but steady. "I thought I'd feel… different. Like I'd wake up and know exactly who I am now."

Adrian's gaze softened. "Maybe that's the point. You don't have to."

Selene laughed quietly, shaking her head. "Since when did you get wise?"

"Near-death experiences. Highly educational."

They stood there for a moment longer, the weight of unspoken words lingering in the space between them. Then Adrian reached out, his fingers brushing against hers, hesitant but real.

Selene didn't pull away.

Not this time.

She squeezed his hand, grounding herself—not because she was lost, but because she was finally *found*.

No sigils. No chains.

Just them.

And the faint hum of a world learning how to live again.

---

The streets of **Nightrift** had changed, yet the echoes of what once was still lingered in the cracks of the pavement and the hushed spaces between conversations. Selene walked through it all, her steps steady despite the weight she carried—not physical, but something deeper. The faint scar over her heart was hidden beneath her jacket, but it burned with a quiet reminder of everything she'd lost and everything she'd fought for.

The city had found a new rhythm. No Council enforcers, no surveillance drones humming overhead. Just people—moving, living, breathing without invisible chains pulling at their every step. She should've felt triumphant, maybe even hopeful. But freedom came with its own kind of emptiness, a hollow space left behind after the battle ends.

Selene found Adrian exactly where she expected him to be.

The old rooftop above a rusted café, overlooking the heart of the city. He sat on the edge, his legs dangling over the side, cigarette burning low between his fingers, though she knew he wasn't really smoking it. Just something to do with his hands. The wind tugged at his jacket, ruffling his dark hair, and for a moment, he looked like the same man she'd met years ago.

But he wasn't. And neither was she.

She didn't announce her presence. Just climbed the rusted ladder and sat beside him, her silence sliding into the space between them like it belonged there.

Adrian glanced over, a small, crooked smile tugging at the corner of his mouth. "Took you long enough."

Selene snorted softly. "I was busy. You know, saving the world."

Adrian flicked the cigarette away, watching the ember die as it fell. "Yeah. Funny how no one tells you what comes after that part."

She leaned back on her hands, staring out at the city. "They don't write stories about it because it's the boring part."

"Is that what this is?" he asked quietly. "Boring?"

She thought about that for a moment, then shook her head. "No. Just… quieter."

Adrian nodded, as if that made perfect sense. They sat in the silence again, letting the city's sounds fill the gaps—the distant hum of life, footsteps below, voices rising and falling like waves.

After a while, Selene broke the quiet.

"Do you ever think about it?"

He didn't ask *what* she meant. He knew.

"Every day," he admitted, his voice low. "What we lost. What we left behind."

Selene traced the scar beneath her jacket, her thumb brushing over the faint ridges. "I thought it would feel different. Like after everything, I'd wake up and know how to be okay."

Adrian turned to look at her, really look at her, his eyes darker than the sky above them. "Are you?"

She met his gaze, unflinching. "I don't know."

He nodded slowly, as if that was the only answer he'd expected.

They didn't need to talk about love. It was there, woven into the spaces between words, etched into the things they didn't say. There was no need for declarations. Just *understanding*.

Adrian pulled a flask from his jacket, unscrewed the cap, and handed it to her without a word. She took it, took a sip, the burn in her throat grounding her more than she wanted to admit.

She handed it back, their fingers brushing for a brief second—a spark, fleeting and fragile, but real.

Adrian's voice was soft when he spoke again. "We saved the world."

Selene exhaled a breath that felt heavier than it should. "Yeah. Now we just have to figure out how to save ourselves."

He didn't have an answer for that.

Neither did she.

But maybe that was okay.

They sat there until the sun dipped below the skyline, the shadows growing long, stretching out like echoes of the past. And for the first time in a long time, Selene didn't feel like she was drowning in them.

She was just *there*.

Alive. Scarred. Still figuring it out.

But there.

--------

The apartment was quieter than Selene remembered.

Dust floated lazily in the slanted afternoon light, particles suspended like tiny echoes of the past. The walls still bore the faint stains of water damage, the cracks tracing spiderweb patterns where old paint had peeled. Her coat hung on the back of a chair, the fabric heavier than it had ever felt, carrying with it the weight of every choice she'd made. She stood in the doorway for a long time, the key still gripped loosely in her hand, even though the door was already open.

She didn't know what she expected to feel—relief, maybe. Triumph, even. Instead, there was just… stillness. No hum of surveillance drones outside the window. No flicker of sigil marks hidden beneath sleeves and collars. The oppressive grip of the Council was gone, their legacy dissolved like ash in the wind. But some things didn't fade so easily.

Selene crossed the room, her steps deliberate, until she stood in front of the cracked mirror mounted above the small dresser—*the same mirror from the day this all began.*

The fracture down the center remained, a jagged line splitting her reflection into two imperfect halves. She stared at it, her own face unfamiliar yet achingly the same. There were faint shadows beneath her eyes, lines carved from exhaustion and experience. The scar over her heart wasn't visible beneath her shirt, but she could feel it there, as constant as her heartbeat.

She tilted her head slightly, studying herself—not just the surface, but what lingered behind her gaze. There was no sigil anymore, no mark of ownership, no tether binding her to anything beyond herself. But freedom had its own kind of weight, and she carried it like a phantom limb.

Her fingers brushed against the cracked glass, cool beneath her touch. She traced the fracture without thinking, her breath slow and steady.

In the silence, her reflection stared back. The same face. The same eyes.

But then—just for a second—*it blinked.*

She hadn't.

Selene froze, her breath catching in her throat. The room seemed to shrink around her, the edges blurring. She leaned in slightly, searching for some logical explanation—*fatigue, stress, a trick of the light.*

But the reflection remained still, its eyes meeting hers with a depth she didn't recognize.

A flicker. A shadow. Gone in an instant.

Selene stepped back, her hand falling away from the glass. She didn't say anything. Didn't call out. Just stared for a moment longer, her heart settling back into its rhythm as if nothing had happened.

Then she turned away.

She picked up her coat, shrugged it over her shoulders, and walked out the door without looking back.

Because whatever remained—whatever the Veil had left behind—*it would have to follow her.*

She wasn't afraid anymore.

# Epilogue
# The Shadow That Remains

The **rain** had finally stopped, leaving the streets of **Nightrift** slick and glistening under the glow of neon signs. Puddles mirrored the city in fractured reflections, warping the reality of a world still learning how to breathe without chains. The Council had fallen, its influence reduced to whispers in dark alleys and the ruins of old power. The sigils had faded, the contracts dissolved, and for the first time in generations, people were free.

But freedom came at a price.

Selene Ward leaned against the railing of a rooftop, high above the heartbeat of the city she had fought to save. Her coat billowed slightly in the wind, but she barely felt the cold. Below, life carried on—people moving through the streets, no longer watched by unseen eyes, no longer marked by invisible brands of servitude. It should have been a victory.

And maybe it was.

But the scars left behind weren't just physical.

Adrian stood a few feet away, hands in his pockets, watching the same city unfold beneath them. He hadn't said much since the night the Council crumbled. Since the Veilborn had **retreated.** Since Selene had come back.

Or most of her, at least.

He glanced at her now, his gaze searching. "You okay?"

Selene exhaled a slow breath, her fingers brushing the faint scar over her chest. The place where her sigil had been. The mark was gone, but sometimes, when she closed her eyes, she could still feel it pulsing.

"Define 'okay,'" she murmured, offering a faint smirk.

Adrian huffed a quiet laugh. "You're alive. That's a start."

She nodded, though she wasn't sure if 'alive' was the right word. Something had changed in the Veil. When she had torn her contract apart, she had expected oblivion, expected to disappear like the others before her. But something **had pulled her back.**

Or someone.

She turned slightly, catching her reflection in a windowpane across the alley. Her own face stared back at her, the same sharp eyes, the same tired expression. But just as she started to turn away, it happened—**the reflection blinked.**

She hadn't.

Selene's breath hitched. The air around her thickened. For just a second, the reflection's lips curved—not in a smirk, not in exhaustion.

In amusement.

"Selene?" Adrian's voice grounded her. She blinked, snapping her gaze away from the glass, her pulse thudding hard in her chest.

"I'm fine," she lied.

He didn't believe her. But he didn't push.

They stood in silence for a moment longer, the weight of the past few months pressing against them.

Finally, Adrian spoke. "What now?"

Selene considered the question.

What came after you saved the world?

What came after **undoing centuries of control, after dismantling a system that had been built on the bones of those who came before?**

The city below them was proof that life **moved on.** People rebuilt. They adapted. They survived. But her story wasn't over.

And she wasn't sure if that terrified her or thrilled her.

Selene turned to Adrian, the flickering city lights casting long shadows across his face. "We find out what's left. And we make sure no one ever tries to rebuild what we destroyed."

Adrian tilted his head slightly. "And if they do?"

Selene's lips quirked into something that wasn't quite a smile.

"Then we burn it down again."

The wind shifted, carrying the distant sounds of laughter, of conversations, of a world learning how to exist without a cage.

Selene took one last look at the city before turning toward the rooftop's exit. She didn't know where the next path led.

But for the first time in a long time—

She was ready to find out.

And in the window behind her, **her reflection lingered just a second too long before following.**

www.ingramcontent.com/pod-product-compliance
Ingram Content Group UK Ltd.
Pitfield, Milton Keynes, MK11 3LW, UK
UKHW040904240225
455493UK00001B/218